PENGUIN  CLASS

T0200961

THE SONG OF KIỀU

NGUYỄN DU (1766–1820) was born into turbulent times. His mother (a singer-songwriter) and his father (a poet, historian and senior figure in the Lê dynasty that had ruled Vietnam for centuries) died before he reached his teens; the Lê dynasty itself was overthrown in 1789 by a peasant uprising. When that uprising was in turn crushed (1802), Nguyễn Du reluctantly accepted a diplomatic post in what would become Vietnam's final dynasty. Outwardly respectful to his new masters, he wrote *The Song of Kiều* secretly, as an act of private rebellion. It remains perhaps the greatest masterpiece of Vietnamese literature.

TIMOTHY ALLEN was born in Liverpool in 1960, and worked for many years as an aid worker funded by the Irish government. On a field trip to Vietnam in 1999 with CAFOD, he first encountered Vietnam's national epic, *Truyện Kiều* and began to work on its translation. He currently teaches English at the University of Liverpool, where he lives with his wife Ann Molloy and their children Oisín and Molly.

NGUYỄN DU

The Song of Kiều

A New Lament

Truyện Kiều

(Đoạn Trường Tân Thanh)

Reworked into English by TIMOTHY ALLEN

PENGUIN BOOKS

PENGUIN CLASSICS

UK | USA | Canada | Ireland | Australia
India | New Zealand | South Africa

Penguin Books is part of the Penguin Random House group of companies
whose addresses can be found at global.penguinrandomhouse.com.

First published in Penguin Classics 2019

002

Translation, Introduction and editorial notes copyright © Timothy Allen, 2019

The moral rights of the translator have been asserted

Set in 10.25/12.75 pt Minion Pro
Typeset by Jouve (UK), Milton Keynes
Printed and bound in Great Britain by Clays Ltd, Elcograf S.p.A.

A CIP catalogue record for this book is available from the British Library

ISBN: 978-0-241-36066-8

Contents

A Note on Naming Systems

The Vietnamese original on which this English version is based goes by many names. Its author, Nguyễn Du (1766–1820, pronounced very roughly 'nwin zoo') had initially intended to call it *Đoạn Trường Tân Thanh* (斷腸新聲), which elsewhere[1] I have translated as 'Broken Heart, New Lament', although other possible renderings include 'New Accents of a Heart-Rending Song'[2] or 'The New Scream that Cuts your Guts'.[3] No matter how we translate it, *Đoạn Trường Tân Thanh* is certainly an enigmatic title. Its first publisher changed the name to the more straightforward *Kim Vân Kiều Tân Truyện* ('A New Story of Kim, Vân and Kiều') before printing it in Hanoi around the time of Nguyễn Du's death; it became an instant posthumous success. Today in Vietnam the poem is usually called *Truyện Kiều* ('The Story of Kiều'), or *Kim-Vân-Kiều*, or simply *Kiều*, or a variation of those names. I have called this version *The Song of Kiều*, celebrating the musicality and the importance of song in Kiều's story, along with a subtitle of *A new lament*, both as an echo of Nguyễn Du's original intention and to preserve the sense of newness (*tân*, 新) that was common to the author's and the original publisher's preferred names for the text. *Kiều*'s earliest readers would have seen Nguyễn Du's poem as a new Vietnamese version of an old Chinese story.

Kiều was originally written in *chữ Nôm* (字喃, literally 'southern characters'), the logographic Vietnamese system that is based on Chinese script. Today, modern Vietnamese is written in *chữ Quốc ngữ* ('national language script'), a Portuguese-inspired alphabet with special diacritics to indicate tones and additional sounds. Throughout these notes and the Introduction, when I talk about 'the original' I normally mean the *chữ Quốc ngữ* version (whose title looks like this: *Truyện Kiều*), even though strictly speaking the original was written in *chữ Nôm* (so that the title looks like this: 傳翹).

Nguyễn Du's *Kiều* (1820) is based on a Chinese novel, *Jīn Yún Qiáo Zhuàn* (金雲翹傳, 'The story of Jin, Yun and Qiao', publication date uncertain; my guess is around 1659–60), which in turn is a brazenly creative account of actual historical events in 1556. Translators into a third language, beyond Chinese and Vietnamese, are obliged to make a nuanced decision about how to present the story's proper nouns – that is, the people and places in the story. When I first published three or four extracts from my version of the poem, back in 2009–10, I chose to leave almost all names in Vietnamese, reasoning that this would reinforce the impression that these English-language extracts were based on a Vietnamese original. In preparing this book-length version, however, that system no longer felt appropriate – on the contrary, it seemed likely to confuse, particularly alongside an account of the historical and geographical (i.e. Chinese) background of the story.

To make life even more complicated for translators, we face the question of how to transcribe Chinese names for English-speaking readers. For several decades, the usual way to make logographic Chinese more accessible to English speakers involved the Wade-Giles system, which meant that (among other items) Beijing is spelled 'Peking'. Increasingly this system has been replaced by Pinyin (literally 'spelled sounds'), normally in a simplified version which omits Pinyin's tonal diacritics. The system I have adopted for *The Song of Kiều* is to keep most of the character names (apart from those whose Chineseness seemed especially significant) in Vietnamese, while giving the place names in simplified Pinyin. My intention is to give a sense of Vietnamese characters existing in a Chinese setting, which seems closer to the feel of the original.

There are three (or possibly four) characters in *Kiều* who have real-life historical antecedents. The Jiajing emperor[4] (Pinyin) is mentioned, but does not appear; his name would be spelled 'Chia-ching' in Wade-Giles and 'Gia Tĩnh' in Vietnamese. The lead negotiator for the Ming is called 'Hu Zongxian' in Pinyin; he would be 'Hu Tsung-hsien' in Wade-Giles and 'Hồ Tôn Hiến' in Vietnamese. The pirate Xu Hai is called 'Hsü Hai' in Wade-Giles and 'Từ Hải' in Vietnamese. The fourth character is Kiều herself – my personal guess is that she is almost completely fictitious. To distinguish between her various manifestations, I use 'Cuiqiao' to refer to the (possibly real) concubine of Xu Hai; 'Qiao' to refer to the character in *Jīn Yún Qiáo Zhuàn*; and I use italics to distinguish between *Kiều* the text and Kiều the woman in *Truyện Kiều*/*The Song of Kiều*. I trust that all this will be far less complicated for the reader than it is for the writer.

The oldest versions of the Vietnamese text present the poem as a single whole, without any kind of chapter breaks. The editor or translator of the poem into whatever language – hoping to make it more accessible to the reader – has therefore to make a decision as to how to divide it up. There are several Vietnamese editions of the poem, and more than fifty translations into other languages. Most translators make their own choices as to where to break for a new section: Lê-Xuân-Thủy's prose translation, for example, contains twenty-seven chapters, plus an epilogue, and presents the first sestet separately, as a kind of epigraph; Vladislav Zhukov's translation, which of all English-language versions is the most faithful to the poetic form of the original, presents it as twenty-eight cantos. I have chosen to follow the divisions used in Huỳnh Sanh Thông's translation, which I greatly admire, and which divides the story conveniently into six manageable sections of roughly equal length.

As for my numbering system, I have unconventionally fronted each section with half a dozen words translated from Vietnamese into English. The words are based on the Vietnamese numbers from one to six (*một, hai, ba, bốn, năm, sáu*), taking the uninflected letters for each number as a base, and then looking up in a standard bilingual dictionary the meanings of as many variants as I could find by adding diacritics.[5] I confess that this originates from my own notes as a struggling poet-translator coming to grips with the rudiments of the Vietnamese language; as I looked at my notes on the page, they seemed to give not only an indication of the complexities of the tonal system, but also a kind of unexpected and slightly haphazard insight into Vietnamese society itself.

NOTES

1. See the 2008 Stephen Spender Prize for Poetry in Translation: http://www.stephen-spender.org/_downloads_general/Stephen_Spender_Prize_2008.pdf.

2. La Société Indochine Films et Cinémas records that a 1924 film of this name was directed by E. A. Famechon; unfortunately no surviving print of this early cinematic *Kiều* is known to exist.

3. See, for example, the 'Lecture Notes from Mr Tien' (1998) at <https://www.deanza.edu/faculty/swenssonjohn/kieu/#tien>

4. In the opening lines of the poem, I have called him simply 'Jiajing', even though, strictly speaking, these formal titles apply to the reign, so that he should properly be referred to (as here) as 'the Jiajing emperor'. The stress is on the first syllable, so that it should be pronounced JAH-jing, as a near rhyme for 'badging'.

5. I used the Thế Giới *Việt Anh–Anh Việt* dictionary, published in Hanoi in 1999.

Introduction

A perfect icon needs to be poised somewhere between knowledge and vast ignorance. And what we get with [Bobby] Sands is that we get enough knowledge that we can identify with him as a person but also, you know, he is so young . . . There is so little of his life that you can fill in all those blanks in any way that you want. Well, that's just the way mythology works.

Fintan O'Toole in the TV documentary
Bobby Sands: 66 Days, 2016

I turn to these works of art because after the official memos and speeches are forgotten, the history books ignored, and the powerful are dust, art remains. Art is the artifact of the imagination, and the imagination is the best manifestation of immortality possessed by the human species, a collective tablet recording both human and inhuman deeds and desires. The powerful fear art's potentially enduring quality and its influence on memory, and thus they seek to dismiss, co-opt, or suppress it.

Viet Thanh Nguyen, Nothing Ever Dies, 2016

1. FROM DWARF PIRATES AND PULP FICTION TO *KIỀU*

Over the past two centuries, *The Song of Kiều* has become one of the central myths that have helped fortify, entertain and inspire the people of Vietnam. In his historical background to Huỳnh Sanh Thông's ground-breaking translation, Alexander Woodside calls *Kiều* 'a kind of continuing emotional laboratory in which all the great and

timeless issues of personal morality and political obligation are tested
and resolved (or left unresolved) for each new generation. Western
readers who are curious about Vietnam and the Vietnamese may well
gain more real wisdom from cultivating a discriminating appre-
ciation of this one poem than they will from reading the entire library
of scholarly and journalistic writings upon modern Vietnam which
has accumulated in the West in the past two decades.'[1] Professor
Woodside wrote those words in 1983, since which time many excel-
lent works on Vietnam have been added to that ever-expanding
library; it is testament to the power of Nguyễn Du's masterpiece that
his point still holds.

I knew almost nothing of the book's significance when I first
bought a softback copy of *Kiều* from a Hanoi street vendor late in
1999. He was working the main drag that circles Hoàn Kiếm lake; all
around him were other adults and children who were buying and
selling postcards, calendars, chewing gum and newspapers – the
kind of thing that is sold in markets and city streets throughout the
developing world. This particular salesman was selling copies of
just three books: a trilingual edition (in Chinese, Vietnamese and
English) of the prison diaries of Hồ Chí Minh;[2] a Soviet hagiogra-
phy of Hồ Chí Minh; and the Thế Giới 1994 edition of *Kiều*.[3] I
bought all three.

The Thế Giới *Kiều* combines Michael Counsell's English transla-
tion on the verso facing Nguyễn Du's Vietnamese (in *chữ Quốc ngữ*
script) on the recto page; it contains also a sprinkling of inked illus-
trations by an uncredited artist. The volume is cheaply bound and
the print is occasionally smudged, but two decades later my own
copy is still going strong: the pages may be yellowing, undulant and
slightly translucent, but they haven't fallen out of their binding. The
Thế Giới *Kiều* is cheap, popular and very readable, and it became
my introduction to the fabulous world of *Kiều*.

Borges claims that it is impossible to read a classic for the first
time: our literal first encounter is our actual second, since we have
already heard so much about any given classic text before we open
it.[4] For me, *Kiều* proved an exception to that Borgesian rule, since
I knew practically nothing about the poem when I first opened it,

although the locals would soon help me appreciate the nation-defining significance it holds for the people of Vietnam. Working for a development NGO, my brief visit took me all over the country, and wherever I went – from the slums and suburbs of Hồ Chí Minh City, through the rainforest villages of the Mekong Delta and the mountainous hamlets of the centre and north, to the corridors of power in Hanoi – I found people who were happy to talk about this 200-year-old poem. From my starting point of near total ignorance, I had begun to sense what so many visitors to Vietnam had discovered long before me, namely that even a basic knowledge of *Kiều* provides the traveller with a rewarding pathway into Vietnamese society.[5]

I learned also that *Kiều* encompasses several stories in one. On the one hand, there is the swift-flowing, lyrical and subversive poem that became such an instant and lasting popular success in Vietnam (and the impatient reader is welcome to skip this Introduction and dive straight into it). On the other hand, there are the various stories of that story: how a fictional heroine took centre-stage in the retellings of an event involving factual men, for example; and how later still, a diplomat-poet transformed that Chinese heroine and those Chinese events into something quintessentially Vietnamese.

Other paradoxical features strike the reader from the opening pages. Although its immediate source material is a historical novel written in unremarkable Chinese prose, *Kiều* is written in Vietnamese *lục bát* verse,[6] an epic undertaking comparable in its ambition to *The Divine Comedy* or *Paradise Lost*,[7] rich with allusions to classical East Asian literature, folklore and philosophy; and it was clearly intended by its author (just as it continues to be understood by its readers) as a kind of embodiment of the Vietnamese spirit. Many commentators have noted that, beautiful though the poem looks on the page, it is more beautiful yet when read aloud or chanted or sung – and indeed it has inspired many musical adaptations.[8] Nevertheless it is a work which, from its opening page, draws attention to its own physicality ('This manuscript is ancient, priceless, / bamboo-rolled, perfumed with musty spices . . .') and invites its reader simply to relax and enjoy it ('Sit comfortably by this good light, that you may learn / the hard-won lesson that these characters contain'). The final couplet returns to that material fictionality and extends it, commending Kiều's story to the reader's own life and personal struggles. *The Song of Kiều* is a work that celebrates the vital and sensual pleasures of reading.

It shares also the several paradoxes common to all works of fiction, one of the most obvious of which is that fiction claims to tell a kind of truth via the unlikely method of making things up. This is compounded in the case of *Kiều* by its being based on well-documented historical events, away from which the narrative has spectacularly freewheeled. This is perhaps why so many modern readers find themselves being drawn into a thorough investigation of the historical and literary antecedents of the poem.[9]

The elements leading to the creation of Nguyễn Du's *Kiều* can be quickly stated, roughly as follows. In the sixteenth century, China's southern coastal areas were being tormented by *wokou* (literally 'dwarf pirates', the Ming dynasty's catch-all term for bandits and sea raiders).[10] In 1556, the Ming's Supreme Commander in the south, Hu Zongxian, offered one pirate chief a poacher-turned-gamekeeper post with the imperial government, on condition that he surrendered. Xu Hai accepted, but Hu Zongxian did not fulfil his promise: Xu Hai was ambushed and killed (or more likely he killed himself). A similar proposal was made a couple of years later to a pirate called Wang Zhi, with a similar result, after which the pirates stopped listening to offers. Over the next few years, as this story was retold, the focus shifted to one of Xu Hai's supposed concubines, a talented singer called Cuiqiao, who was reckoned to have convinced her man to accept the government's calamitous offer. When this account was finally published more than a century later in the form of a popular historical novel (*Jīn Yún Qiáo Zhuàn*, by the pseudonymous Qīngxīn Cáirén[11]), Qiao had become its main protagonist, and the negotiation between Hu Zongxian and Xu Hai had been relegated to a minor episode towards the end of her many adventures. A century and a half later still, that old half-forgotten novel was picked up by Nguyễn Du, who translated it into transcendent Vietnamese poetry.[12]

That, in a nutshell, is how the story of *Kiều* came about. We can find in it, perhaps, a misogynist trope familiar to us from Hebraic parables of women from Eve through Delilah to Judith, of the woman as the strong man's weakness, as the quickest and most treacherous route to his vulnerability. In *Kiều*, however, this idea is turned on its head. First, although Kiều persuades Từ Hải to accept the deadly offer, she does so in good faith. Second, although she blames herself, nobody else follows suit – in fact a Buddhist wise woman later explains how Kiều's intervention has fortunately if unwittingly saved 10,000 lives. Third, the treachery is presented as being entirely on the part of the Ming official who made Từ Hải an offer he had no intention of keeping.

Within the great sweep of Chinese history, this was of course a very minor incident. Locally, however, it had a dramatic impact, reflected in the wide range of contemporary documents that carried accounts of it – sometimes supporting and sometimes contradicting each other – supplemented by oral retellings of those same events. Qīngxīn Cáirén (a pseudonym meaning 'the Pure-Hearted Talented Man') used these written and spoken accounts as source material in creating *Jīn Yún Qiáo Zhuàn*, a popular novel in the talent-beauty style, published more than a century later,[13] in or around 1660. The timing of its publication is significant for two reasons: more than four generations had passed, so that the events of 1556 were now beyond the direct memory of the oldest people around; and the Ming dynasty itself had collapsed (in 1644), so that when the book was published in the early years of the Qing dynasty, *Jīn Yún Qiáo Zhuàn* was expressing a complicated perception of the Ming that was part-critical and part-loyal. This in turn resonated with Nguyễn Du a century and a half later, as he was mourning a fallen dynasty of his own.

The talent-beauty (*cáizǐ jiarén*) novel was a briefly popular genre that seems to have begun towards the end of the Ming dynasty and then flourished in the early years of the Qing. The typical plot was escapist and predictable; to modern eyes it seems flagrantly sexist, with its equations of *talent* = *male* and *beauty* = *female*. A talented young man meets a beautiful young woman: they fall in love. A sleazy older man – usually a prominent government official – plots against the lovers, creating obstacles which they must overcome if they are to meet again. They overcome them; the official is executed; the couple marry and have three children; they live happily ever after.

While Western readers today might find the form trite and formulaic (and the genre has long since fallen out of fashion in China), it was the talent-beauty novels, rather than the Six Classics,[14] which were the first Chinese works to be published in Europe: three of them had appeared in French, English and/or German in the eighteenth and nineteenth centuries, long before even a partial translation of a bona fide classic (*Dream of the Red Chamber*, part of *The Story of the Stone*) was published in English in the 1890s.[15] European readers of those days expected novels to focus on a central character and to follow a straightforward plot line; the talent-beauty novels fit this bill better than the Six Classics, which contain a multitude of characters and a complex network of storylines – a novelistic form that would not be attempted in Europe until much later.[16] In theory, this single-protagonist preference could have made both *Jīn Yún Qiáo Zhuàn* and *Truyện Kiều* more accessible to English-speaking readers familiar with the picaresque adventures of Moll Flanders or the dilemmas facing Samuel Richardson's Pamela. In practice, neither work reached Europe before the twentieth century. This is perhaps because Qiao's story abandons too many conventions of the standard talent-beauty pattern, in which the heroine may be threatened with a fall in status, but she shouldn't actually become a prostitute; she may be threatened with violation, but she shouldn't actually get raped. It seems also that when early European readers first became aware of *Truyện Kiều*, they dismissed it as a mere translation from Chinese.

As Eric Henry observes, *Jīn Yún Qiáo Zhuàn* takes the form of a talent-beauty novel bookending a picaresque adventure story. Its account of the events of 1556 is shoehorned into the adventure story to provide it with a couple of false endings (first, Qiao's meting out of justice to those who have either helped or tormented her; second, the downfall of Xu Hai) before the final return to the conventionally happy ending of the talent-beauty storyline. *The Song of Kiều* preserves all these main elements of its Chinese source novel, with occasional and significant modifications. The following three points may serve as examples:

1. In *Jīn Yún Qiáo Zhuàn*, when Jin first sets eyes on Yun and Qiao, he falls in love with (and inwardly vows to marry) not one but both of them.[17] In *Kiều*, however, although Kim clearly likes both sisters, it is unequivocally Kiều who captures his heart.

2. Jin and Qiao first converse through a crack in the mud wall that separates their houses. Jin uses an iron bar to make the crack bigger and squeezes through it, only to find that Qiao, who has waited passively and demurely while he was doing all this, chastely refuses his embrace. In *The Song of Kiều*, however, it is Kiều herself who takes the initiative at that stage of their relationship, hitching up her sleeves, unlocking the gate and running across the grass towards her lover.

3. Much later in the story, when Lady Huan appeals for clemency by explaining what provoked her to abduct and torture her rival, Qiao spares her life – but not before she has had Huan stripped naked, hung from a roof beam by her hair and flayed with four horse-whips.[18] In *Kiều*, Huan's counterpart Lady Hoạn makes a similar appeal, but in this case Kiều frees her without further punishment. In the former text, we sense perhaps something of the salacious prurience of the pulp-fiction writer; in the latter, we find Nguyễn Du's sense of compassion for the plight of women in general, alongside a vindication of the healing power of well-chosen words, both of which themes permeate *The Song of Kiều*.

One of the ways in which *Kiều* follows *Qiáo* closely is in recounting the vigour and boundless wandering of their eponymous heroines, yet this is an aspect in which *Jīn Yún Qiáo Zhuàn* itself differs starkly from the historical source materials. Most of the early accounts of 1556 make no mention of any concubine; when they do, they usually speak of concubines plural, in contrast with the monogamous relationship described in both *Qiáo* and *Kiều*. In fact, an early account (by Mao Kun) provides a detail that reminds us that the woman whose adventures compose *The Song of Kiều* definitely could not have existed in Ming-era China. He describes how Xu Hai's concubines were carried from the battlefield on the backs of sturdy pirates.[19] This detail reinforces for us what should have been obvious, namely that a sought-after, prestigious Chinese concubine of 1556 would certainly have had bound feet. Yet Kiều by contrast is an all-action heroine: scaling walls, riding horses, walking for miles. During the Jiajing reign, those activities would have been beyond the scope of most women from middle- and upper-class families, in which the painful practice of binding daughters' feet to keep them cripplingly tiny was widespread. Not even the idyllic scene at the beginning of the story (in which the sisters and their brother stroll hand-in-hand beside a pretty brook) would have been possible, because in real life, for a cloistered northern family like the Wangs/Vươngs, both girls would have had to be carried for any distance further than a couple of hundred metres. The practice of foot-binding never spread to Vietnam, and was less common in the south of China, where the story originates, but in the northern provinces where the early parts of the story take place, foot-binding would have been all but universal for a girl of Kiều's social class.

None of this does much to address two of the commonest questions raised by readers coming to *The Song of Kiều* for the first time. First, why is there so little correlation between the historical events and the story that sprang out of them? Second, why is this supposedly canonical work of Vietnamese literature entirely set in China? What makes *Kiều* anything more than a lyrical translation of an old Chinese novel?

Whatever the manifold failings of the Ming, their documentation systems for the period were second to none, and the events of 1556 are so well recorded that it is possible not only to work out a plausible hypothesis about what really happened, but also to map out from those origins a likely path to the story you hold in your hands. As for the second question, we will need to look first at the histories both of China and Vietnam, which will help us see the connections Nguyễn Du was expecting his readers to make between the Ming and the Lê.

2. A BRIEF HISTORY OF THE MING

The 1820 publication of *Truyện Kiều* rescued an old Chinese myth from oblivion, sending it into the future that we ourselves inhabit. Nevertheless, Nguyễn Du's masterpiece remains but a single retelling of that continuing myth – the most brilliant link in the chain perhaps, but we should not leave aside the chain as we admire the link. At one level, *The Song of Kiều* is one of those timeless classics that seem to exist outside of time, in a fictional Never-Never Land 'where peach trees always bloom beside a fairy stream', while at another level, it represents sixteenth-century China filtered through *fin de siècle* Vietnam. At its most literal level, however, the story takes place over a fifteen-year period (roughly 1542 to 1557[20]), setting it in the middle of the Jiajing reign (1521–67), which itself means the middle of the Ming dynasty (1368–1644). Yet the publication of *Jīn Yún Qiáo Zhuàn* (*c.*1659–60) makes it equally a story from the early Qing (1644–1912), a tale of mourning for a lost world, at once wistful for and highly critical of a fallen dynasty, infused with a strong sense of what might have been. After the fall of Beijing, there remained several pockets of Ming resistance in the south of China, and this resistance was particularly strong in the region where the closing events of the Qiao/Kiều myth are set; a Beijing-based author writing about the Ming, even pseudonymously, was playing a dangerous game. The resonances of both these periods (middle Ming and early Qing) appealed strongly to Nguyễn Du at the turn of Vietnam's nineteenth century, and all those elements – the keening, the sense of loss and of a destiny that cannot be changed, even the precariousness surrounding publication – are all to be found in *The Song of Kiều*. In order to understand how these resonances work for a writer in nineteenth-century Vietnam, we should first think about the Ming; to understand the Ming, we need to think about China itself.

Many countries make for themselves a claim of exceptionalism – of being different from all other nations – yet none has so strong a claim as the nation we call China. The sheer enormity of its population continues to dwarf all others, apart from India – even after rigorous and successful efforts to curb its exponential growth. Another distinctive feature of China is the notion contained in the name it gives itself: Zhongguo (中國), meaning the Middle Kingdom, the central state. Originally this was a purely administrative description of the Zhou midlands, but it came to be used as the name of the whole empire, placing China literally at the centre of the world, with peripheral nations considered in terms of their relation to the central core. Before 1945, Vietnam was known as Annam (安南), meaning 'the pacified south' just as Vietnam (越南) itself means 'southern people'. It goes without saying that in both cases 'south' means 'south of China'. This unshakeable faith in its own centrality partly explains China's chameleonic ability to metamorphose whenever its dynasties are overthrown: throughout its long history, whenever one dynasty decayed, another took over, taking on the mantle of the new leaders of China. Its capital cities moved about, reflecting these shifts in political power, and its borders were fluid – in vain they built a Great Wall to try to fix them – but the notion of Zhongguo as the Middle Kingdom persevered. Even when Genghis Khan invaded China – subsuming it into the biggest land-based empire the world has ever seen – his own regime became accepted as the next Chinese dynasty, albeit one of foreign origin. Genghis's grandson Kublai chose a dynastic name that was descriptive of his empire's ambitions, rather than of its ethnic origins – calling it 'Yuan' (元) meaning 'great', from the opening lines of the *I-Ching*: 'great, like the beginning of the world'.

This was the first version of 'China' that Europeans encountered – the century-long Mongol interlude in a largely Han Chinese history that had continued for roughly four millennia.[21] When Marco Polo[22] brought back his astounding stories of the mighty land of Kublai Khan, whose capital was at Khanbalik (meaning 'Khan city') and whose summer palace was at Xanadu (today spelled 'Shangdu', 'upper capital'), his readers were amazed. Europeans of those days thought of themselves as living through stormy and ignorant times; nostalgic for the radiance of the classical past, they were hopeful that their descendants might be born into a more enlightened era.[23] By contrast, the land that was then called Cathay sounded full of marvels: paper, coal, eyeglasses and banknotes, for example, all of which would later become part of the regular fabric of European life.

Europeans were not to know that finding a non-Chinese dynasty in charge of China was a real anomaly, but nevertheless it was no coincidence, given that Genghis Khan's Mongol armies had opened up the Silk Road and thus enabled the Polos to travel along it. Once the Ming had overthrown the Yuan, that transcontinental road closed over once more, and Europeans would have to explore sea routes if they wanted to reach Cathay again. The Ming had little interest in exploring the world's extremities – they fully expected foreigners to want to visit China, rather than the other way around.

After Kublai Khan's death, the Yuan dynasty was weakened. Having swept across the two continents of Asia and Europe in a blaze of military glory, the rulers found it difficult to maintain such a large empire, even after dividing it into various fiefdoms, each ruled by a different descendant of Genghis Khan. Their custom of ranking citizens according to ethnic origin, with the Mongols at the top, proved unpopular with local populations everywhere. Their mismanagement of the economy led to widespread famine; and their only answer to popular discontent was to attempt to quash it by military force.

The mighty Mongol empire was eventually overthrown by southern peasants whose campaign was financed by their merchant neighbours – the same pair of communities that two centuries later would provide the source for the Qiao/Kiều myth. The heroic founder of the Ming dynasty was a peasant, Zhu Yuanzhang (1328?–98), whose parents and siblings had starved to death – he escaped the same fate only by joining the local Buddhist novitiate. When that monastery was burned down by Yuan troops bent on crushing a local uprising, the young monk vowed revenge. He raised a rebel army and established his base at the southern city of Jintian, using this for an assault on Khanbalik, which he soon captured, razing the Khan's palaces, and thus founded the Ming dynasty. One of his most far-reaching early administrative decisions was to rename both those cities: Jintian became 'Nanjing' – the southern capital – while Khanbalik became 'Beijing' – the northern capital.[24]

We can see in Zhu Yuanzhang shades of Từ Hải from *The Song of Kiều* – the southern rebel versus the northern empire. We can see also the north–south duality that would become a feature of the Ming empire and – by coincidence, but even more strongly – a feature of Vietnamese life also. This sense of a delicate north–south balance, and of military tensions spilling across the divide, would be one of those many elements of the Qiao myth in which Nguyễn Du would find strong parallels with his home country.

It was also Zhu Yuanzhang who named his new dynasty 'Ming'. The ideogram Ming (明) combines the pictograms for sun (日) and moon (月) to convey a sense of brightness.[25] When the Ming themselves were overthrown in the 1640s, the invading Manchu chose for their dynasty the name Qing (清), combining the pictograms for water (水) and blue (青) to create a composite that means 'purity'. There is a scissors-paper-stone logic to this naming progression. The ancestors of the Manchu (the Jurchen) had founded the Jin dynasty (1115–1234) that had flourished for more than a century until its overthrow by a Mongol-Song coalition. Jin (金) means 'gold', named after the Gold River in their homeland, and of course gold is a metal and therefore can be melted by the fiery brightness of the Ming. Fire, however, is extinguished by water. By changing Jin to Qing, the Manchu were figuratively confirming their victory over the Ming. In addition, the famous festival celebrated at the opening of *The Song of Kiều* is known as Qingming (literally 'pure brightness', or the Feast of Pure Light). By choosing the name 'Qing', the Manchu were ensuring that their name would for ever precede that of the Ming in one of the most important dates of the Chinese calendar.

All of this should give a sense of the importance of names and of interlingual wordplay in East Asian cultures – something which is almost impossible to convey in a translation. It illustrates too one advantage of logographic languages (which use ideograms to convey meanings) over alphabetic languages (which use letters to convey sounds). Speakers of different languages can look at the same ideogram and understand the same meaning, even though they will pronounce it quite differently.[26] This gives those cultures a direct insight into each other's literatures in a way that – without knowledge of each other's languages – Europeans cannot match. Vietnamese, Cantonese and Mandarin speakers can look at each other's writing and are able to understand its meaning instantly, even though they may not have an inkling how their neighbours would pronounce it.[27]

Before Vietnam achieved its independence by expelling the Southern Han from its territory in 939, China had occupied Vietnam for three lengthy and roughly consecutive spells, lasting for more than a thousand years. Although Chinese rule had often been brutal and oppressive, it had also brought many practical and cultural benefits to its southern neighbour. Practical Chinese innovations that helped Vietnam's population to grow included rice-growing, irrigation and improved farming methods; cultural innovations included writing, art, literature and philosophy; politically, after throwing off Chinese rule, Vietnam adopted a system that mirrored the dynastic successions of the Middle Kingdom.

Vietnam shared some of China's weaknesses also. Fortunately for its girls and women, the practice of foot-binding never caught on in Vietnam; unfortunately for its boys, eunuchism did. This barbaric practice (in which the testes and often the penis were severed with the swipe of a razor, creating a class of castrated men who were then entitled to perform special functions at the imperial court) began as a punishment, inflicted on criminals, dissidents and prisoners of war. For obvious reasons, these eunuchs were then considered ideal candidates for managing and supporting harems.

The practice was developed still further, however, to address a particular problem perceived to be inherent in the notion of hereditary succession. Most Chinese dynasties were created by a successful military leader who had overthrown the previous dynasty. The question of what would happen when that leader died was solved by primogeniture: the notion that the emperor would pass the mantle to his eldest son, who would later pass it to his own eldest son, and so on, a system that was intended to prevent infighting between rival candidates for the throne.[28] However, large empires are difficult to run single-handed and therefore emperors aimed to surround themselves with a team that was both talented and loyal. Since their own life experience had taught them that talent often outlasts loyalty, they selected this team from two groups: Grand Secretaries, chosen for their expertise in (and fidelity to) the conservative Confucian code; and eunuchs, whose ambitions would be limited to this lifetime alone, without the complication of descendants. Some commoners, driven by desperate poverty or simple ambition, would even castrate themselves or their own sons in the hope of securing a post as an imperial eunuch.

This created a complex triangle at the head of a Chinese dynasty that looked something like this:

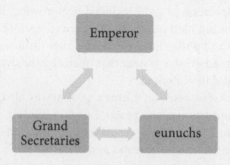

Power would shift along the sides of the triangle depending on who could outmanoeuvre whom in the machinations of the imperial court. This system meant also that Chinese dynasties tended to begin with a flourish – at their point of greatest triumph – and would then begin the long, slow slide towards disintegration. It takes skill, planning and courage to replace a powerful but decaying empire, but once the founders of the new dynasty are gone, power rests with their descendants, who find themselves at the head of a powerful empire without having had to work hard to get there.[29]

Another feature endemic to Confucian systems is the primacy given to agriculture over trade. This notion underpins imperial distrust of mercantilism, particularly when the trade is international, creating a tension (between the empire and its own merchant class) which drives the plot of the Qiao/Kiều myth and which also led to the terminal decline of the Ming, Qing and (in Vietnam) the Lê dynasties. Confucius divided society into four economic strata as illustrated below:

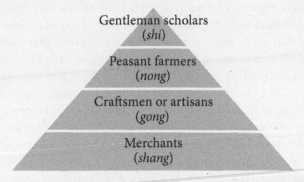

Gentleman scholars
(*shi*)

Peasant farmers
(*nong*)

Craftsmen or artisans
(*gong*)

Merchants
(*shang*)

While this promotion of agriculture no doubt gave a healthy fillip to food-growing, it proved disastrous for trading, particularly at a point in human history when international trading vessels from as far afield as Europe were beginning to appear on the horizon. Zhu Yuanzhang had funded his rebellion against the Mongols through the promotion of international trade; when he became the first Ming emperor, however, he introduced a sea ban (海禁, *haijin*) designed to stamp out the very funding mechanism that had helped sweep him to power. Whatever his motives, the effect was gradually to impoverish the mighty Ming dynasty over the course of several generations, while other nations around the world were becoming wealthier. Vietnam's Lê dynasty followed a similar policy, with equally calamitous results.

The Qiao/Kiều myth offers an imaginative exploration of how the ordinary law-abiding citizens of China and Vietnam were affected by the tensions surrounding the trading community, and how women in particular were disproportionately affected. Both novels begin with the heroine's father being unjustly accused of a trivial crime: Qiao's father is accused of harbouring thieves, while Kiều's father is accused of not having repaid his debt to a silk merchant. In each case, Qiao/Kiều understands that she must sacrifice herself to save her family. The problems of trade-gone-wrong result from the interactions of men; the solutions depend on the self-sacrifice of women.

Chinese emperors for many centuries had been aware of the enormous potential wealth that could be amassed via maritime trade, but for that very reason they were keen to ensure that exchanges took place in a centralized imperialist fashion: peripheral nations were obliged to bring tribute to the imperial court, and would receive gifts in return. The idea that private individuals could organize trading voyages of their own raised the prospect that the emperor's own subjects would start to gain wealth that might rival that of the court.

This problem had become acute by the mid-sixteenth century, particularly along China's south-eastern coast. European ships were now regularly appearing in Chinese waters, and Europeans were seeking to establish trading posts in and around Ming territory. The Ming's sea-ban policy was justified as one of necessary self-defence – local traders were referred to as 'pirates' and 'Japanese' even though most of them were Chinese merchant families from coastal towns in the regions immediately south of present-day Shanghai.[30] From the merchant-pirates' point of view, this policy often entailed their being effectively exiled to islands off the coast of mainland China, whence they could plan trading missions to and from Japan and the Chinese coast. Often these traders saw themselves as loyal to (and would crave acceptance from) the imperial court; sometimes they would accrue sufficient wealth to raise private armies and navies that could be used for both raiding and piracy.

This ambivalent attitude towards empire – part loyal, part resentful – underpins the events of 1556. It is also an ambivalence that clearly resonated with the author of *Jīn Yún Qiáo Zhuàn*, and later still with Nguyễn Du, who at the beginning of the nineteenth century was experiencing his own complicated feelings towards the shifting dynasties of Vietnam. The sea-ban policies effectively meant that the Chinese and Vietnamese empires were actively opposing the creation of wealth – by their own citizens – that eventually could have helped their nations to thrive. On the western side of the Eurasian landmass, much weaker European monarchs were growing in strength precisely by sponsoring the kind of trade-bearing sea voyages that the Ming and Lê were trying to stamp out. This is the context in which the events of 1556 take place.

The Jiajing reign (1521–67)

The Song of Kiều opens in the middle of the reign of the Jiajing emperor, enthroned at the age of thirteen to replace a young cousin who had died in his twenties from complications that followed a drunken boating accident. The Ming had reached that stage in their dynasty where it had become normal to give absolute power to children, with disastrous results. The Jiajing emperor's self-destruction would take a while longer than many of his predecessors – he was almost sixty when he died – but he never really outgrew the prolonged adolescence that the imperial system unintentionally provided for its emperors. Even in his teenage years, the Grand Secretaries and eunuchs found it difficult to manage or manipulate him. The young tyrant quickly established a court system in which promotion was earned by those who supported the emperor's personal agendas, while more pressing affairs of state were neglected.

One matter that had become increasingly urgent by the 1520s was the issue of piracy in the south. Because of the ban on sea trade, legitimate Chinese merchants were losing vast sums to their piratical neighbours, who not only conducted international trade alongside their piracy, but also frequently raided the undefended southern coasts around Fujian and Zhejiang. Formerly law-abiding local merchants were therefore starting to construct ocean-going ships both to defend themselves and to flout the sea ban. The Grand Secretaries were deeply concerned, and began to suggest to the emperor possible solutions, such as an easing of the ban on overseas trade. Jiajing refused to consider this, seeing it as an affront to his imperial majesty that Ming subjects should question his law. In 1529, he ordered the destruction of all seaworthy vessels belonging to Chinese merchants. This tipped the balance of naval power disastrously in favour of those who were outside Ming jurisdiction – foreigners and pirates. Thus the Jiajing emperor unwittingly laid the groundwork both for the demise of his own dynasty and for the chain of events that would eventually inspire *The Song of Kiều*.

His management style was petulant and obtuse. He would make bad decisions and then, realizing that things were going badly, would reverse the decision, presenting the reversal as his own brilliant solution to a problem that – though he never acknowledged it – was of his own making. He hated both the north-west Mongols and the south-east pirates, but his mismanagement of the economy meant that his army lacked the resources to defeat either group. After every military defeat, he would execute scores of his own troops, sometimes including officers, generals and even Ministers of War, hoping that fear would goad the survivors towards a future victory. Instead, of course, it simply weakened his army still further.

His lack of personal charm may be deduced from the fact that in November 1542 his own palace ladies conspired to try to kill him. He took his favourite concubine to the royal bedchamber; as soon as he had fallen asleep, she and her attendants withdrew. A maid then gave the signal to the others, who shuffled into his bedroom on their broken feet, armed only with hairpins. They took a silk cord from the bed curtains, slipped it around his neck and pulled tight while stabbing at his groin with their pins. The needles were not long enough to do serious damage, and the slip-knot intended to choke him to death failed to complete its job. In the commotion, the palace guards rushed in and saved his life. He remained in a coma for several hours, and then awoke, coughing up blood. The women were all executed, overseen by the empress; the emperor later blamed his wife for not having spared his favourite concubine. Despite her apparent involvement in triggering the assassination attempt, he would have preferred to have kept her.

From that point on, the Jiajing emperor withdrew from the formal life of the court and refused to spend another night in the Forbidden City. Taking some replacement concubines with him, he moved out to the Palace of Everlasting Longevity, situated in a park in the west of Beijing, where he spent the rest of his days.

By the mid-1550s, the emperor was pushing fifty and had become seriously concerned about his own mortality. He was not consoled by the thought of the posthumous immortality granted all Ming emperors; his intention was to live for ever on this earth. Hoping to discover the elixir of eternal youth, he employed a Taoist alchemist to create a range of aphrodisiacal compounds based on a mixture of red lead and white arsenic. A court official who warned the emperor of the dangers of these supposed aphrodisiacs was arrested and tortured to death.

Lead and arsenic do not provide eternal youth, but in small doses they do produce insomnia, stomach complaints, mood swings, dementia and eventual death. The Jiajing emperor displayed all of these symptoms in his final years, as he steadily poisoned himself. In his final months, his attendants would place peaches on his bed while he slept, explaining that the immortals had dropped them from heaven during the night. He died in 1567 at the age of fifty-nine, having been severely demented for more than a year.

The fall of the Ming dynasty

On the face of it, the opening lines of *The Song of Kiều* look back fondly to that Jiajing reign as a kind of golden age. The final reign of the Ming era – which is when the folk retellings of the Kiều story were heading towards their first novelization – was just as chaotic and just as profligate.

The Ming's main antagonists throughout most of their dynasty had been the Mongols to the north-west and the pirates to the south-east. Their eventual downfall however came from the north-east, where the Manchu – a semi-nomadic people related to the Mongols – lived beyond the Great Wall, close to the border with Korea. The death-throes of the Ming dynasty were overseen by the Chongzhen emperor, whose managerial style was similar to that of Jiajing, but by now that style was unsustainable, as the dynasty was finally running out of money. When the Manchu captured Beijing, they found its coffers were empty and its soldiers had not been paid for five months.

Court officials in the Chongzhen era had become adept at telling the emperor what he wanted to hear. Anyone attempting to tell him the truth was likely to be executed on the spot, or – worse still – slowly tortured to death. As the Manchu invasion was gathering momentum in May 1643, senior Grand Secretary Zhou Yanru volunteered to take personal command of the garrison at Tongzhou, north of Beijing. When he arrived there, he found that the Manchu had already moved on, and so he opened a bottle of wine and began concocting fake battle reports. The emperor, delighted to read these stories of how comprehensively the Manchu had been routed, recalled Zhou Yanru to Beijing, rewarding him with an aristocratic title. However, these fictitious victories could not compete with the string of factual defeats. As the Manchu closed in on Beijing, in January 1644, the emperor told Zhou that he no longer believed he had won all those battles, and commanded him to commit suicide. By 25 April, the enemy were within the city gates and were being welcomed by the local citizens.

The Chongzhen emperor then committed an atrocity that encapsulates the worst of a dynasty whose citizens saw castration as a career move and foot-binding as a sign of social status. He had his servants prepare nooses and summoned his two most important wives along with their children. He told Queen Zhou that as the first lady of the empire she would have to die with the Ming. She answered: 'I have been married to you for eighteen years, and yet you have never listened to a word I said. That's what has brought us to this situation today. But since you command me, I have to die.' Both wives then hanged themselves. He then set about his own children with a sword, explaining that they should not have been born into an imperial family. He stabbed his six-year-old daughter to death, but succeeded only in severing the left arm of the fifteen-year-old Princess Changping. Other women and children also died in a combination of murders and forced suicides. Blaming incompetent Ming officials for having ruined the empire, the emperor then hanged himself on Jingshan Hill, behind the Forbidden City. He left a note reminding whoever found him that he was the Son of Heaven. He was thirty-three years old.[31]

The mysterious case of the dissident critic

The publication of *Jīn Yún Qiáo Zhuàn* perhaps fifteen years later thus serves as a kind of coda to the Ming era. It opens with a halcyon image of the empire at peace, the beautiful girl meeting the talented boy during the feast of Qingming, exactly as the contemporary romances fantasized – and then sets about dismantling that illusion. The girl is sent headlong into a corrupt and conniving world that almost destroys her, where the best hope for justice comes from a benevolent outlaw. That rebel's defeat at the hands of the empire comes about not by his being outfought or outwitted, but through a blatant act of deceit and abuse of power. What permeates the novel is a sense of the structural misogyny of the empire and how its appalling brutality disproportionately affects women.

There is, however, another significant element to *Jīn Yún Qiáo Zhuàn* – *The Song of Kiều* omits it entirely – which gives that Chinese novel an unintentionally comic if curiously postmodernist feel. The main storyline is accompanied by a commentary purportedly by Jin Shengtan (金聖歎, 1610?–61), who to this day remains one of the most influential critics in China's long literary history. At the head of each chapter, 'Jin Shengtan' presents a short note praising the quality of the writing and commenting upon the morality of the novel's characters.

Critics of our own day are uncertain about the publication date of *Jīn Yún Qiáo Zhuàn*, although all agree that the real Jin Shengtan did not write the commentary signed with his name. For one thing, the novel itself is simply not very well written, and so it is hard to imagine why such an acerbic critic would have recommended it. For another, the chapter introductions do not resemble his usual style of analysis, which typically involved interlinear readings deconstructing the subtle techniques used by the great writers. Fake or not, the very existence of the commentary is useful to us because the life and tragic death of its alleged author sheds some light on that elusive publication date.

Jin Shengtan was born into poverty around 1610. His original name was Jin Renrui – he chose the name Shengtan (meaning, roughly, 'the sage's sigh') as he began to carve out a career elucidating great works of past literature. He played a key role in framing and redefining the Chinese canon, notably elevating both the novel *Shuihu Zhuan* (*Water Margin*) and the play *Xixiang Ji* (*Romance of the Western Chamber*), via a series of idiosyncratic and often brilliant close readings, peppered with insults targeting previous critics[32] for not having noticed these points before. His originality and candour proved hugely popular – the young Qing emperor Shunzhi (1638–61) commended him publicly in 1659.

Given that *Jīn Yún Qiáo Zhuàn* names him as a co-author, Jin Shengtan's death in 1661 gives some clues as to when the book might have been written. One of the following unlikely scenarios must be true, although all three raise difficult questions:

1. Jin Shengtan did write the commentary – but in that case why did he praise such a mediocre work, without explaining his reasoning, and in a style quite different from everything else he wrote?

2. The author or publisher of *Jīn Yún Qiáo Zhuàn* wrote a self-promoting commentary while Jin Shengtan was still alive, and ascribed it to the most-respected critic of the day – but in that case why did not Jin Shengtan simply deny having written it? Or at least, why was the author/publisher unafraid that he might deny it?

3. The author/publisher put Jin Shengtan's name to the fake commentary after he was dead – in which case, why did nobody point out that a dead man could not have written the commentary?

The circumstances of the critic's death make the third option even less likely. In January 1661, the newly appointed magistrate of Jin Shengtan's hometown (Suzhou) took draconian measures to recover back taxes. He flogged farmers in their own fields; he sequestered grain that had already been paid for and demanded the owners pay a second time for it to be released. Many local people were unhappy about this new turn of events and they turned to prominent figures, including Jin Shengtan, for help.

The young Shunzhi emperor, who had seemed open to a pro-intellectual approach within the fledgling Qing empire, died from smallpox in February 1661, at the age of twenty-two. More than a hundred students gathered for three days of mourning at Suzhou's Temple of Confucius, which gave them the opportunity to discuss their grievances about the new magistrate and devise a plan of action. On the fourth day of mourning, they presented a jointly signed letter to the provincial governor calling for the magistrate's dismissal. Eleven of their leaders were promptly imprisoned. A second group, including Jin Shengtan himself, protested against these arrests and they were arrested also. The governor falsely reported that these intellectuals had rioted, and he condemned seventeen of them to death on grounds of treason. The new Manchu/Qing regime was determined to show the local Chinese literati that complaints would not be tolerated. Jin Shengtan was beheaded in August, his property was seized and his son was exiled to Manchuria.[33]

Thus began the long 'literary inquisition' that followed the death of the Shunzhi emperor. The Qing regime's murderous distrust of literati would continue for more than a century – the next three emperors (Kangxi, 1654–1722; Yongzheng, 1678–1735 and Qianlong, 1711–99) were so long-lived that they lasted to the cusp of the nineteenth century, and all three emperors severely persecuted poets and prose writers. For example, during the Yongzheng reign, the poet Xu Jun (徐駿) wrote the following couplet: 'It makes no sense for the breeze to keep turning the pages, since it cannot actually read.'[34] The breeze here was taken to refer to the Qing dynasty, and therefore Xu Jun was summarily executed. A poet and teacher named Xu Shukui (徐述夔) wrote a poem in praise of his late father; unfortunately the Qianlong emperor, when it came to his attention, took this eulogy as a personal insult. In 1778, he ordered that the dead Xu's corpse be exhumed and mutilated, and all his children and grandchildren beheaded.

There was probably never a good time to publish a novel in medieval China, since Ming and Qing authorities alike mostly distrusted the form and frequently sought to ban it. However, the 1650s, when a young, outward-looking emperor was actively seeking to involve local intellectuals in his regime, would seem to have been a more favourable decade than the 1660s.[35] Jin Shengtan published his commentary on *Xixiang Ji* in 1656, and the young emperor publicly praised his work in 1659. It seems a fair guess, then, that the *Jīn Yún Qiáo Zhuàn* commentary was written sometime around those dates. On the other hand, by the spring of 1661, Jin Shengtan had been publicly condemned as an enemy of the state. After his death, his cousin gathered together his papers and published his collected works (reprinted in 1744) without mentioning *Jīn Yún Qiáo Zhuàn*. Given these circumstances, I think the most likely date for publication would have been 1659 or 1660, when Jin Shengtan's reputation was at its height, but without giving him too much time to deny having written the commentary, since he was arrested in May 1661 and was executed three months later.

Transition to *Kiều*

Considering the paranoia of the Qing emperors regarding any criticism from their Han Chinese subjects, the mere survival of *Jīn Yún Qiáo Zhuàn*, with its supposedly 'Jin Shengtan' commentary, is remarkable. It not only survived, however, but clearly remained popular for several decades, running to several editions; a Japanese version was published in the 1740s. Partly this is because it was presented as a historical novel, set in the middle Ming period and detailing the tribulations of an honest young woman during that era, so that whatever criticisms of the establishment it implies, those criticisms are directed at the Ming, not the Qing. It slips into other genres too, of course, with its talent-beauty and adventure-story frameworks, and the middlebrow quality of its writing perhaps accounts for both its popularity and its good fortune in slipping under the Qing's inquisitorial radar. It is one of those 'slick and banal novels', as Eric Henry describes them, which were popular with ordinary readers but which neither commanded the respect of the intelligentsia nor aroused the suspicions of the Qing elite.[36]

That might have been enough to see *Jīn Yún Qiáo Zhuàn* through its first century or so, but if that was all there was to it, I doubt that any of us would still be reading the Qiao myth nearly 500 years after it first sprouted. There lies beneath its surface something that a reader as perceptive as Nguyễn Du identified immediately, sensing the layers of ambiguity and complexity that spoke directly to the Vietnam of his own day. In reworking the myth, he was able to draw out its lyricism and its allusiveness, creating a poem that, two centuries later, continues to surprise its readers with its freshness and modernity.

As for the fate of *Jīn Yún Qiáo Zhuàn* itself, from the 1980s onwards Chinese scholars such as Lin Chen (born 1928) and Dong Wencheng (born 1941) have discussed 'the Qiao phenomenon' – the curious situation whereby everyone in Vietnam knows about *The Song of Kiều*, but almost nobody in China knows the story of Qiao. *Jīn Yún Qiáo Zhuàn* had fallen into obscurity in China by the late 1950s when scholars first began to draw attention to the Vietnamese *Kiều*, comparing it favourably both to Cao Xueqin's *The Story of the Stone* and Alexandre Dumas *fils*' *The Lady of the Camellias*. Conversely, although *Kiều* is very well known throughout Vietnam, its readers are often surprised to find that it is based on a historical event, and that characters such as Hồ Tôn Hiến and Từ Hải had real-life antecedents.[37] These factual origins of the fictional legend will be considered next.

3. THE BETRAYALS THAT INSPIRED
THE SONG OF KIỀU

The Jiajing emperor does not personally appear in *The Song of Kiều*: he is mentioned by name in the opening lines as part of the idyllic description of the peaceful empire, and again, more incidentally, where Kiều describes Kim's luckiness in life in terms of '[treading] the golden path / towards the emperor's door' or where the narrator emphasizes the prestige of Hu Zongxian ('When he set out from court, the emperor himself / pushed the chariot'). Kiều's naive impression of the emperor is clear also from her description when she persuades Từ Hải to accept the fatal offer: 'The emperor is generous as the rain. / His law keeps the northlands peaceful, / and all his subjects are thankful to him.' There is a sense here of the Jiajing emperor as a wise and benign but distant figure, yet the truth is that while certainly the Jiajing emperor was far removed from his people's suffering, he himself was the direct cause of much of it. Driven insane by the absolute power thrust upon him since childhood, he was a murderous solipsistic thug.

By contrast, Hu Zongxian (胡宗憲, Hồ Tôn Hiến in Vietnamese, 1512–65) is presented as the main villain of *The Song of Kiều*. At the very moment when Kiều seems to have found peace and happiness with Từ Hải, Hu is appointed as the new Ming officer in charge of the south-east provinces, and he sets about achieving by trickery what could not have been achieved by military force: the defeat of the mighty and benevolent rebel warlord. 'Hu Zongxian' in *Kiều* is emblematic of a whole class of Ming officials whose corruption, greed and laziness were rightly seen as exacerbating their people's suffering, although in the real Hu's case this is probably unfair.

In his home village of Kengkou, Anhui province, a different story is told today. There, Hu Zongxian is still celebrated as one of the region's most successful sons, having been rewarded by the Jiajing emperor for suppressing piracy in the south-east; locals tell also how he was later betrayed and died in ignominy, only to be posthumously rehabilitated by a later emperor and given the ceremonial name Xiang Mao (襄懋), meaning 'Splendid Assistance'. The official history of the Ming dynasty lists him as one of its most brilliant and loyal supporters. His reputation grew still further early in the current century when one of his direct descendants, Hu Jintao (胡錦濤, born 1942), became President of the People's Republic of China (2003–13). This provincial family, from an obscure mountain village, has thus made a dramatic impact both on the Ming dynasty and on the modern Communist Party.

There are elements of truth in both accounts of his life, and yet both probably overstate the importance of Hu Zongxian's role in defeating Xu Hai. The events of the middle Ming are well enough documented that it is possible to pick our way through those conflicting accounts and work out a likelier story of what really happened in the 1550s. As might be expected, most of the explanation for what went wrong can be found in the self-destructive machinations of the imperial court itself.

Many court officials – particularly those with roots in the south-eastern coastal provinces – understood that the sea ban on international trade was counter-productive and should be relaxed, or even abandoned altogether. They had also become adept at managing upwards, persuading the emperor towards a particular course of action by convincing him that the change of plan was in fact his own idea. However, this tactic itself created a loophole that was ruthlessly exploited by one official in particular: the notorious Yan Song (1480–1567), who realized that, whenever one of his colleagues was attempting to trick the emperor into reversing his own policy, all he himself had to do was point out the trick and the emperor would quash the proposal, punish the offender and be grateful to Yan Song. Thus he was able to connive his way to the position of Senior Grand Secretary – effectively the emperor's right-hand man. Naturally this also made him many enemies at court, who would attempt to denounce him.[38] To subvert this, he befriended the lowly clerk whose task it was to receive all letters of complaint to the emperor – Zhao Wenhua (1503–57). Zhao was able to intercept all criticism aimed at Yan Song and pass it directly to his sponsor. Alongside the volatile Jiajing emperor himself, Yan Song and Zhao Wenhua were in large part responsible for the disastrous events of the 1550s.

Zhao Wenhua was corrupt, dishonest and unreliable. On a couple of occasions, he had been reprimanded for being drunk at court, although he was temporarily protected by his relationship with Yan Song. A native of Zhejiang, he knew also that the emperor's sea ban and anti-piracy policies were hopelessly misguided. He began to discuss with Yan Song a strategy for solving the problem, rightly believing that whoever succeeded in opening up those southern ports to international trade was certain to become exceedingly rich.

A sea battle in the late 1540s gives an indication of the scale of the problem that faced the conspirators. A local admiral in the southeast, Zhu Wan, following the emperor's direct orders, constructed a large and powerful navy, leading it in March 1549 to attack a consortium of merchant vessels anchored off the coast of Fujian. Many ships escaped; of those he captured, he found they contained not Japanese pirates but a mixture of Chinese and Portuguese traders. He executed ninety-six Chinese and banished the Portuguese. The Chinese traders, however, had friends at the imperial court and Zhu was impeached for having carried out the executions without waiting for the proper authorization. Zhu Wan committed suicide before the impeachment could proceed. In one of those extraordinarily self-destructive acts that became such a feature of middle Ming governance, the imperial troops then sank the navy which Zhu Wan had so carefully assembled, by way of posthumous punishment. Meanwhile Wang Zhi (1501–59), one of the traders who had managed to escape capture, took over the leadership of the trading consortium, which turned increasingly towards piracy. Piracy returned bigger profits than legitimate trade, and since both were punishable by death it was no riskier. With the Ming navy safely scuttled, Wang Zhi grew richer and more powerful – his irresistible rise in fact resembles that ascribed to Từ Hải in *The Song of Kiều* – and he would become one of the key players in the events of 1556.

Back in Beijing, Yan Song and Zhao Wenhua had identified the rising young star of provincial diplomacy, Hu Zongxian, as a key ally to help them solve the pirate problem. A fellow southerner,[39] Hu had earned a reputation for solving regional problems creatively through a hands-on approach; he had also distinguished himself in battle, fighting off a Mongol assault on Beijing and crushing a rebel uprising in what is now Hunan province. Yan Song proposed that the three men divide their responsibilities like this: Hu Zongxian would be given the new post of Supreme Commander of the south-eastern coastal provinces; Yan Song would remain at the imperial court, convincing the emperor of the rightness of their strategy; Zhao Wenhua would be a go-between, overseeing military strategy on the pirate coast, while regularly reporting back to Beijing. All three agreed that in the short term it would be necessary to negotiate with the *wokou*, and that in the long term the ports would have to be opened up to international trade. The Jiajing emperor, of course, was adamantly opposed both to negotiation with those he called 'sorcerer pirates', and also to the very concept of international trade. The three pro-trade allies would have to proceed very carefully.

The Ming court was at this time in serious danger of losing control of the south-east provinces of Jiangsu, Zhejiang and Fujian. Sinking part of their own imperial navy had ceded marine dominance to the pirates, who were increasingly becoming powerful on land also. Ming troops who followed Beijing's orders to engage in combat usually found themselves badly outnumbered, and they would retreat to their barracks while the pirate-bandits pillaged the countryside before returning to their island bases. This pattern provided the historical basis for the latter episodes of *The Song of Kiều*, except that the real 'Lord of the southern people' was not Từ Hải, but Wang Zhi.

Wang Zhi remained a reluctant pirate. Since escaping from Zhu Wan's ill-fated attack on the merchant junks, he had become the undisputed leader of a loose consortium of traders, smugglers, pirates and bandits. A talented linguist, he was able to negotiate in several languages, using this skill to acquire for his troops the superior firepower of European musketry.

Throughout those years, however, his main aim was to persuade the Japanese and Chinese governments to permit legitimate trade. Patrolling the coastal waters off Zhejiang and Jiangsu in a show of good faith to the Chinese authorities, he tracked down several minor pirate gangs who were tormenting the coast and handed them over to the Ming. He argued that if the government would only open up their ports to legitimate trade, he would be in a position to eradicate piracy entirely. The Ming response was to arrest Wang Zhi's wife and mother, insisting that he eliminate piracy immediately if he wanted to see them again.

When Hu Zongxian arrived in the south-east to take up a post as a provincial governor, one of his first actions was to release those two women from prison as a sign of good faith, and to open negotiations with Wang Zhi. The new Supreme Commander offered the pirate chief a post with the Ming navy; in return, the pirate chief instructed his consortium to halt all raids on the Chinese coast. He also explained regretfully that one of his subordinates, Xu Hai, had already planned an attack on the coast (scheduled for April 1556) and it was too late to call it off. Apart from that minor detail, the negotiations had started well.

Xu Hai (徐海, Từ Hải in Vietnamese) was a very different character from his *Song of Kiều* namesake. A former Buddhist monk (his temple was on the south bank of the Qiantang river, which plays such an important role in *Kiều*), he had been persuaded by his uncle to leave the monastery and join Wang Zhi's consortium. He had risen swiftly through the pirate ranks, giving himself the grand title of 'Great General Sent by Heaven to Pacify the Oceans'. He was also something of a loose cannon: when Wang Zhi began taking action against his fellow pirates, Xu Hai tried to assassinate him, a situation that was only resolved through the intervention of Xu Hai's uncle. Hu Zongxian began to look at ways to use diplomacy both to isolate Xu Hai and to make him a similar offer to that already accepted by Wang Zhi.

As it turned out, however, a problem on the Ming side derailed this plan. The pro-trade strategy was about to go badly wrong, in the unlikeliest way imaginable. Three decades of the Jiajing policy of opposing pirates, bandits and traders by force had resulted only in a series of defeats, but in 1556, a newly appointed general, Zhang Jing, finally succeeded in achieving a substantial victory.

Zhao Wenhua had been in the south, expecting to report back on the usual series of military defeats, which would have helped him to convince the emperor that it would be necessary to change tack. When he visited Zhang Jing's garrison, he found a general refusing to attack the pirate bases (which had recently been constructed on the mainland coast) until reinforcements arrived. Zhao Wenhua ordered Zhang Jing to attack immediately and was rudely rebuffed; he wrote an angry missive to Beijing, denouncing Zhang Jing as a coward and an embezzler.

Zhang Jing, however, had been telling the truth; he was simply waiting for the right moment to attack. As soon as the reinforcements arrived, he launched a devastating assault on the pirate bases, capturing almost 2,000 bandits. News of the unexpected victory arrived in Beijing at roughly the same time as Zhao Wenhua's diatribe against Zhang Jing. Yan Song, thinking on his feet, made a decision that would soon backfire: he claimed the victory was really the work of Zhao Wenhua and Hu Zongxian (further claiming that the latter had personally led the troops on the battlefield), denounced Zhang Jing as a liar and demanded he be summarily executed. Despite Zhang Jing's protestations, he was beheaded. It had become commonplace for the Ming to execute their own officers following a military defeat; now they had beheaded one of their most talented generals after he had won them a rare and substantial victory. Zhao Wenhua, who had contributed nothing except to falsely denounce the winning general, was rewarded with promotion to Minister of Works.

Yan Song and Zhao Wenhua were at the peak of their success, but they had also overstepped the mark. Everyone in the south-east knew who had really won the battle, and more accurate accounts of Zhang Jing's victory began to trickle into Beijing. There was a growing realization at court that Yan Song had engineered the death of a loyal and successful general in order to pursue his own nefarious ends.

This was a moment that should have called for careful consideration and judgement from the Jiajing emperor. Unfortunately, his main preoccupation in 1556 was searching for the secret of eternal youth: he was busily scouring fairy stories for any mention of plants that had made people younger or helped them live for ever. He compiled a list of 1,500 such plants and sent his servants to travel the length and breadth of China looking for them.

This precarious situation is almost certainly what really sealed Xu Hai's fate. Hu Zongxian had to think fast. He had been given credit for winning a battle that he didn't even know about, while the general who had really won it had just been beheaded. He already had a gentleman's agreement with Wang Zhi, and he was part way through negotiations with Xu Hai. The emperor's insistence on military solutions to piracy and banditry seemed to have been momentarily vindicated. Hu Zongxian decided to cut his losses: he abandoned the negotiations and ambushed Xu Hai. Xu Hai and his troops held out for a week, but (because they had trusted Hu Zongxian so completely) they had allowed themselves to become hopelessly outnumbered. In a death that prefigured what would happen to the fictional Qiao/Kiều, Xu Hai drowned himself in a river running alongside the battlefield.

A worse betrayal would soon follow, as the political situation worsened for Hu Zongxian's former allies in Beijing. The gates to the Forbidden City had burned down earlier in the year, and four months later there was still no sign of any new gates. The emperor demanded to know why the new Minister of Works had not yet replaced them. Yan Song and Zhao Wenhua now had plenty of enemies at court, who were quick to point out that timber intended for the gates had been diverted towards the construction of an extension to Zhao Wenhua's personal mansion in Beijing. The emperor issued a warrant for Zhao's arrest; Yan Song's own position was in serious trouble also. Before Zhao could be exiled, he died – whether of natural causes or not is unclear.

By this stage, Hu Zongxian was already part way through negotiations with the pirate chief himself. Wang Zhi had sailed into Zhejiang, unconcerned by what had happened to Xu Hai, the hothead who had recently tried to kill him. Nor did he even really see himself as a pirate; he was a legitimate businessman who was happy to put his navy at the empire's disposal, provided they would open up their ports to international trade. He was sightseeing on the West Lake when Hu sent troops to arrest him.

Wang Zhi spent the next two and a half years writing furious letters from prison, protesting his innocence, while Hu Zongxian tried to figure out ways to release him. Hu ran out of ideas and Wang ran out of luck – in December 1559 Wang Zhi was beheaded; even on the morning of his execution, he was still expecting to be pardoned and released. Over the next few years, pirate activity increased – there was no point attempting any further negotiations, and the pirate leader who had striven to keep his men in check was now dead.

The truth was thus far messier than the fictional retellings that followed it. It was also an ending that satisfied nobody. By the end of January 1567, everyone involved in those ill-fated *wokou*–Ming negotiations – the pirates, the Ming officers, even the emperor himself – was dead and the Ming dynasty was in terminal decline.

Having executed Wang Zhi, Hu Zongxian set about trying to exonerate himself from the charge of negotiating with pirates. To rehabilitate his reputation, his friend and confidant Mao Kun was co-opted to create a version of events that would explain away the evidence. The events of 1556 seemed the most difficult to explain, and therefore Mao Kun produced an account designed to show that everything which might have looked like appeasement was actually a cunning attempt to persuade Xu Hai to drop his guard. For example, when accusers complained that Hu Zongxian had sent a banquet to Xu Hai's camp, Mao Kun explained that the rice and the wine had both been poisoned before delivery. The proof of the pudding, according to Mao Kun, was that the pirate ended up dead.

As propaganda, this proved only partially effective. Hu Zongxian avoided impeachment in the short term, but he was continually faced with accusations of being part of the Yan Song clique. Within a couple of years, he was arrested on a minor charge and thrown into prison, where he committed suicide by poison.

Mao Kun's account also mentions the names of Xu Hai's two concubines, Cuiqiao and Lushu, both former singing girls with the family name Wang (implying that they may have been sisters). Apart from being carried away from the camp the night before the battle (which reminds us that they would both have had bound feet), their role is simply to point out, weeping, the place where Xu Hai drowned himself.

A slightly later account, by Xu Xuemo, shows how local people were starting to modify Mao Kun's account of his friend's actions.[40] The two concubines have become conflated into one (Cuiqiao), who is starting to develop some of the characteristics that we will recognize from *The Song of Kiều*. For example, Xu reports that she had started life as a prostitute in Linzhi, whence she had escaped from a brothel run by a woman named Ma. Her relationship with Xu Hai seems particularly complicated – he kidnaps her from Haishang, but then falls in love with her; she attempts to trick him in the hope of escaping; afterwards she regrets her trickery because she belatedly recognizes that he was a good man; and therefore she drowns herself in the Qiantang. Commenting on his own story, Xu Xuemo praises Cuiqiao for two acts of supposed loyalty: (1) betraying the pirate showed loyalty to her country and (2) drowning herself showed loyalty to the pirate. There are several elements of the tale that we recognize from *The Song of Kiều*, but there are also too many contradictions for us to see Xu's Cuiqiao as a believable character.

Nevertheless, we can find in his anecdote some indication of how the oral myth was developing. A local storyteller, Hua Laoren, is named as the source of many of the word-of-mouth accounts Xu Xuemo had heard from the people of Haishang. Hu Zongxian is openly mocked as lascivious and untrustworthy; Xu Hai is seen as a mule-headed bully who falls for the woman he abducted. Set against the violent backdrop of the middle Ming, this anecdote offers some clues about what ordinary people really thought about the imperial world they lived in. Hearing accounts of these lethal arguments between greedy, self-important men, their sympathies were entirely with the woman who had been caught in the crossfire. Lack of available detail about her biographical background was no discouragement; instead, it allowed storytellers to give free rein to their imaginations.

4. A BRIEF HISTORY OF VIETNAM

By now we have seen at least three of the historical avatars of the charismatic rebel leader Từ Hải, who plays such a prominent role in the closing sections of *The Song of Kiều*. First there is the founder of the Ming dynasty himself, Zhu Yuanzhang, who rose from poverty to end the Mongols' Yuan dynasty; and then there are the pirates Wang Zhi and Xu Hai, the latter giving his name to the character.[41] Just as Western readers today might find echoes of Robin Hood or Ned Kelly in the character of Từ Hải, so Nguyễn Du, when he first picked up a copy of *Jīn Yún Qiáo Zhuàn*, could see immediately parallels with the Vietnam of his own day, which at a stroke offered him three further examples of 'virtuous and charitable thieves'[42] in the shape of the three revolutionary brothers who had risen from obscurity to divide up Vietnam between them: Nguyễn Nhạc (?–1793), Nguyễn Huệ (1753–92) and Nguyễn Lữ (1754–87). Their short-lived dynasty, named after their home village of Tây Sơn, collapsed soon after they died, separately and unexpectedly, but each apparently of natural causes – Lữ in his early thirties and Nhạc and Huệ at about the age of forty.

Although the brothers' family name was 'Nguyễn' they are commonly known by the name of their village, Tây Sơn (literally 'Western Mountains' and pronounced roughly, 'tay shurn'), to distinguish them from the Nguyễn Lords who were the first targets of their militant uprising. The same family name is shared, of course, by Nguyễn Du, whose sympathetic portrayal of Từ Hải in *The Song of Kiều* clearly owes a great deal to the Tây Sơn uprising – with its marching southern armies waving enormous red flags – even though his own northern, Trịnh-supporting family (also called Nguyễn!) was traditionally opposed both to the rebellious Nguyễn brothers and to their opponents, the Nguyễn Lords.

Nguyễn Du's feelings about the Tây Sơn dynasty (1778–1802) were evidently complex. At a personal and professional level, the rebellion was disastrous for him and his family, who were all loyal supporters of the Lê dynasty, which the uprising had brought to an end; Nguyễn Du himself refused a post in the Tây Sơn regime when it was offered him – a decision that cost him three months in prison. Yet his portrayal of Từ Hải (the most Tây Sơn-like figure in *Kiều*) is positively heroic, and even the rebel's failings are sympathetically drawn. By contrast, the Ming establishment (analogous to that of his beloved Lê) is shown to be flawed, uncaring and untrustworthy. That ambivalence and ambiguity is part of *Kiều*'s greatness, opening it up to diverse interpretation; it chimes also with Taoist notions of dualistic monism, of the balance of opposites, of yin and yang.

The proliferation of so many Nguyễns on all sides of the Tây Sơn conflict is not so much coincidental as typically Vietnamese. Even today, the family name Nguyễn is shared by roughly 40 per cent of Vietnam's population, giving the surname a disproportionate impact wherever Vietnamese communities are gathered.[43] Its spread throughout Vietnam results primarily from many centuries of political expediency – rulers sometimes forced conquered peoples to adopt the name, for example, while other communities changed their names to Nguyễn during troubled times so as not to stand out from the crowd. This pragmatic desire to blend into the crowd, however, complicates historical accounts, especially where the same family name appears on all sides of the fragmented struggle between the Tây Sơn, the Nguyễn, the Trịnh and the fading Lê dynasty.

The following diagram should help to clarify some of these distinctions, while also illustrating some of the parallel developments of Vietnam and China during the period of the Qiao/Kiều myth.

China	Vietnam	
	Early Lê dynasty (1428–1527)	
Ming dynasty (1368–1644)	Mạc usurpers staged a coup (1527–33) and continued to occupy the north of Vietnam until the 1590s	
	Lê dynasty warlord period in which a puppet Lê emperor was protected by the Trịnh and Nguyễn Lords (1533–1789)	
	Trịnh Lords rule the north	Nguyễn Lords rule the south
Qing dynasty (1644–1912)	Tây Sơn regime (1788–1802)	
	Nguyễn dynasty (1802–1862)	
Chinese Republic (1912–49)	Nguyễn dynasty continues during French occupation (1862–1940)	
	Nguyễn dynasty continues during Japanese occupation (1940–45)	
People's Republic of China (1949 to present)	Socialist Republic of Vietnam (1945 to present)	

It is easy to see how a Lê supporter at the turn of the nineteenth century could find points of commonality with a story from the cusp of the Ming/Qing era in China. Vietnam's Lê dynasty (1428–1789) started out as contemporaneous with the Ming (1368–1644), ran into sixteenth-century difficulties for broadly similar reasons, and arrived at a compromise that enabled it (badly weakened) to ride out those difficulties and thus outlast its larger neighbour. The Lê equivalent of Zhu Yuanzhang was its heroic founder Lê Lợi (c.1384–1433), who founded his dynasty in 1428 by expelling the Ming, thus ending China's fourth and final occupation of Vietnam. Having expelled them, however, Lê Lợi's next action was to petition the Ming to accept Vietnam as a vassal state, on a similar basis to that held by Korea.

This parallelism of Lê with Ming is important to an understanding of *The Song of Kiều*. The longevity of dynasties helps connect the people of East Asia to their own pasts, lending an illusion of eternity to those vanished worlds, to their wisdom and their barbarous practices alike, to their failures and their glittering successes. When Nguyễn Du picked up a book from the mid-seventeenth century, with its mid-sixteenth-century storyline, he saw not only the old history but also the nineteenth-century present, finding the fall of the Lê prefigured in this tale from the days of the fall of the Ming.

Vietnamese dynasties were not always so tightly wedded to primogeniture and Confucianism as their Chinese counterparts, but the conservative Lê dynasty followed a similar pattern to the Ming. In less than a century, the dynasty's heroic founders had been replaced by a succession of all-powerful adolescents, drinking and murdering their way through short, savage reigns. Yet while the Jiajing emperor was tightening his grip on the Ming court, the head of the Vietnamese army decided he had had enough of protecting juvenile psychopaths, staged a *coup d'état* and founded the Mạc dynasty (1527–92). The Lê dynasty was eventually restored to power, some decades later, but the real power from that point on rested with two groups of landed aristocrats – the Trịnh Lords in the north and the Nguyễn Lords in the south. This widened the north–south division in Vietnam, deepening the fault line that the USA would seek to exploit, nearly three centuries later, as it hoped to create a puppet state of its own in the south of Vietnam.

Within Vietnam, the cultural stereotype of northerners is of hard-working, impoverished, literary intellectuals from a mountainous region with cold winters, while southerners are seen as lazy, cunning, jovial, trade-loving people, good at making money, from the monsoon region of the Mekong rainforest. Of course, such cultural stereotypes are neither more nor less true in Vietnam than are equivalent stereotypes elsewhere, but they were established during those centuries of the Trịnh-north versus the Nguyễn-south, and have since been reinforced by those post-Second World War decades of a socialist Việt Minh north counter-balanced with a capitalist, USA-influenced south. The former imperial capital at Huế is located part way between the two; the location of the current capital at Hanoi, combined with the renaming of Saigon to Hồ Chí Minh City, is indication of how strongly the north currently dominates the nation. Nguyễn Du was born into a more evenly balanced country, with a feeble Lê emperor nominally overseeing a society in which peasant discontent was continually rumbling against both the northern Trịnh and the southern Nguyễn.

The Tây Sơn uprising, then, began not as a revolt against the Lê dynasty but against the Nguyễn Lords of southern Vietnam. Nguyễn Nhạc, a young betel-nut trader, was co-opted by the Nguyễn Lords to work as a tax collector. From the outset, though, he hated collecting taxes. Based out of his home village of Tây Sơn, he saw the poverty of the farmers all around him and he understood that taxation was making that poverty worse. One day, he walked out on his job and headed for the hills, where he began raising a rebel army. The Nguyễn Lords sent a larger army after him to demand from him the taxes he had refused to collect.

Nhạc then launched his rebellion with a single act of extraordinary courage and ingenuity, which to Western eyes seems to have come straight from the Homeric playbook. He instructed his followers to put him in a cage and to deliver him to the provincial governor of the local city, Qui Nhơn. They were to claim that they had captured the delinquent tax collector and to ask for a reward.

The governor was delighted, paid them and displayed the caged Nguyễn Nhạc in the centre of town.

That night, Nhạc let himself out of the cage, as arranged, and opened the city gates to his rebel army. By means of this Trojan horse-style ruse, they made short work of the defenders, burned down the barracks and established Qui Nhơn as their base for what would eventually become the conquest of the whole of Vietnam.

It is hard not to be impressed by the inventiveness and the courage of Nhạc's opening gambit. It could so easily have gone wrong, ending his revolt before it began, and yet he trusted that his wit and daring would outmatch the powerful forces of the Nguyễn Lords of southern Vietnam, and he was proven right. He cracked the stone open at its weakest point – that weakness being the arrogance and complacency of a regime that assumed that everyone wanted to pay tribute to it. He ordered his followers to offer himself by way of tribute, aiming to prove that an independent spirit could not be cowed by the crushing weight of imperial power.

From their south-central base, the three brothers expanded to conquer the whole of Vietnam. Carrying huge red banners, the Tây Sơn soldiers terrified their enemies, hissing like snakes as they marched. Having started by enacting a Greek myth, these hissing armies switched to an English legend, gaining a reputation for stealing from the rich and giving to the poor. They sent the southern Nguyễn Lords into exile, crushed the Trịnh Lords in the north and thus ended the Lê dynasty's 360-year-old reign. They divided up the country between them: the most brilliant brother, Nguyễn Huệ, became the Emperor Quang Trung, and took control of the north; Nguyễn Nhạc himself commanded the central region; while the youngest, Nguyễn Lữ, oversaw the south. All three of them died young, however, and their regime was not able to survive the premature deaths of its charismatic founders. In 1802, the Nguyễn Lords returned from exile, defeated the remnants of the Tây Sơn army, and became Vietnam's final imperial dynasty.[44]

With great reluctance, Nguyễn Du accepted a post first as a teacher, then as a diplomat, working for the new Nguyễn regime. Although his loyalties were instinctively with the Trịnh and the Lê, he accepted the humiliation of working for the Trịnhs' traditional rivals because the Nguyễn themselves had overthrown only the Tây Sơn rebels, not the Lê directly. Many northern literati refused to accept this compromise and withdrew to the countryside. Nguyễn Du agreed to work for the southern regime, but he remained deeply troubled by his own decision.

Nguyễn Du had been born into the old imperial citadel of Thăng Long in central Hanoi. His mother was his father's third wife, who had reputedly been a famous singer and musician in her youth. His father, who had been a prime minister in the Lê regime, died when Nguyễn Du was ten, and his mother died three years later. Although orphaned early in life, he maintained a strong sense of loyalty to his parents, and this sense of filial loyalty resonates throughout *The Song of Kiều*.

On an ambassadorial visit to China in 1813, Nguyễn Du encountered *Jīn Yún Qiáo Zhuàn* for the first time. He sensed in Kiều a kindred spirit, just as she herself senses a sister soul when she happens upon Đạm Tiên's grave. Reading that piece of old pulp fiction, with its trite formulae and its conventional frameworks, proved life-changing for this world-weary, middle-aged intellectual. Somehow he found in the story of Kiều an answer to all his doubts, regrets and uncertainties. The act of transforming that unpromising material into a work of art of such lasting beauty is what saved him, and he invites us into Kiều's world, offering the possibility that our own imperfect lives may be enriched – even redeemed – by the clarity of her song.

Commentaries on *Kiều* tend to dismiss *Jīn Yún Qiáo Zhuàn*, with its fake Jin Shengtan chapteral blurbs, as an inferior work, transformed beyond recognition by the genius of Nguyễn Du. Certainly there is truth in this – at the heart of the so-called Qiao phenomenon is the inescapable conclusion that *Jīn Yún Qiáo Zhuàn* simply isn't very good. Specialists may study it as an unconventional example of the talent-beauty novel, or as the otherwise unremarkable source material of *Kiều*, but it no longer attracts a readership beyond that. The judgement of posterity has effectively left *Qiáo* to gather dust, while its Vietnamese incarnation continues to thrive and to attract new readers. Nevertheless, it should not be overlooked that the craftsmanship of the Pure-Hearted Talented Man provided Nguyễn Du with far more promising source material than, say, the self-exculpatory accounts of Mao Kun or the colourful folk stories told by the likes of Xu Xuemo. One feature of this craftsmanship is geographical: the plot is shaped so as to ensure that its characters cover as much of China as possible, effectively knitting a divided nation back together (see the map on p. lxvii). This notion was especially appealing to a Vietnamese poet whose own nation had been shattered by centuries of infighting and discord, and who created in response a vernacular epic that continues to unite Vietnam today, asserting the nation's irrepressible independence of spirit, despite repeated attempts to divide or invade it since.

The travels of the Vietnamese have also continued, especially since those more recent conflicts, so that Vietnam's people are now numbered among the world's great wanderers, with well-established communities in Europe, Australia and North America. The musicologist Deborah Wong once asked the great Vietnamese songwriter Phạm Duy why all his song cycles involved travelling. He answered:

I am the old man wandering, the old man on the road. It is my destiny and the destiny of my people – always moving. The Jews and the Chinese went everywhere, but slowly, gradually. The Vietnamese went all at once – in one day, one hour! *Viet* originally meant to cross over – like an obstacle – to overcome. So this is the essence of the Vietnamese spirit. Now *Viet* just means 'people', though its real meaning is 'the people who overcome, who cross over'.[45]

For the Vietnamese diaspora of the twenty-first century, the figure of Kiều inspires them on their journeys to the ends of the earth: she is the perpetual overcomer, the crosser-over, the wanderer, and her homesick songs of exile are music to the ears of those who have had to travel so far from their beloved Vietnam.

5. THE CREATION OF KIỀU

If *Jīn Yún Qiáo Zhuàn* was, in a sense, protected by its own mediocrity, the same could not be said for *The Song of Kiều*. Nguyễn Du's poem exploded into the cultural life of Vietnam, becoming an instant popular success, and thereafter has been acclaimed by successive generations who have found ways to demonstrate how it supports their own worldview, whether pro-colonial or anti-colonial, capitalist or communist. Early in *The Song of Kiều*, Kiều's brother teases his sister for using another's story to throw light upon her own ('You talk of Đạm Tiên, but weep for yourself'), and it was obvious to *Kiều*'s earliest readers that Nguyễn Du himself was doing exactly that: his retelling of an old Chinese story was offering a critical reflection on contemporary Vietnam. This was not lost on the Nguyễn emperor either, who commented that if the author had not already died, he would have had him executed for treason.

The exact circumstances of *The Song of Kiều*'s composition and publication are unclear. By the end of the 1810s, handwritten copies of the manuscript were already being circulated in Hanoi, where the poet's friend and fellow writer, the teacher Phạm Quý Thích (1760–1825), was using the poem as a basis for discussion with his students. Although Nguyễn Du had been scheduled to make a second diplomatic trip to China in 1820, he fell ill and died in the September of that year, at the age of fifty-five. Phạm Quý Thích then published the dangerous text, giving it the title *A New Story of Kim, Vân and Kiều*.

The creation of the Qiao/Kiều myth thus involves four stages. Initially, there are the official reports produced by Hu Zongxian and Mao Kun, designed to help them avoid punishment for having negotiated with pirates. Second, local storytellers rescued the figure of the woman from that self-serving story, praising her for her fidelity. Third, the author of *Jīn Yún Qiáo Zhuàn* shaped that oral tale into a publishable fiction, adding the frameworks of the love story, the adventure story, the talent-beauty novel, all of which helped make it an ephemeral popular hit, as well as expanding Kiều's story geographically. Finally, that novel found its most extraordinary reader in Nguyễn Du, who not only saw a contemporary resonance in that old myth, but developed ways to tease it out, adding poetry and a wealth of classical allusions, along with comedy to counterpoint the tragedy. An echo of his own mother appears there in the figure of Đạm Tiên, the dead singer whose gravestone the siblings happen upon during the Qingming festival. Lost to Nguyễn Du in childhood, she reappears to him in dreams, just as Đạm Tiên with her ghostly gown becomes a protective figure watching over Kiều.

A distinctively Vietnamese understanding of family runs throughout *The Song of Kiều*. Precise family connections are hardwired into the Vietnamese language system, so that every human being on earth needs to be located somewhere within the speaker's expansive idea of family. This goes far beyond the related way that an English speaker might refer to an elderly man as 'granddad' or to a significant neighbour as 'auntie', or a Spanish speaker might say 'mi hijita' to a child who is not technically their own. Vietnamese speakers, when they meet someone new, immediately have to work out whether to refer to them as 'younger sister' (*em*) or 'older sister' (*chị*), as 'father's older brother' (*bác*) or 'father's younger brother' (*chú*), for example. The founder of modern Vietnam, Hồ Chí Minh, may have been thought of abroad either as an evil communist or as a hero of liberation, but famously within Vietnam he is referred to more avuncularly as 'Bác Hồ' – 'Uncle Ho'. Kiều's difficult early decision to abandon her lover for her family has a special meaning for such a family-centred nation.

In the earliest versions of the story, it is Xu Hai who drowns himself in a river; soon afterwards, this suicide shifts to one of his concubines. By the time of Nguyễn Du's version, Kiều's attempted suicide – throwing herself into the mighty Qiantang river – is thwarted by some of the people she has met during her travels: first, the ghostly Đạm Tiên and then, more practically, she is rescued by the nun Giác Duyên and her hired fishermen. Together with the supernaturally clairvoyant figure of Tam Hợp, these women extricate Kiều from the contaminated world in which a woman is valued for her transient beauty rather than for her talent or her spirit.

Yet those talents are remarkable. Kiều's lyrical ingenuity far exceeds the technical accomplishments of the conventional fictional heroine. Her words serve as a powerful shield, protecting her from the villains who would destroy her and altering the course of the destiny that had originally seemed mapped out for her. Sometimes these words take the form of spoken eloquence: Kiều speaks and those around her are charmed or find themselves altered, their opinions changing, their plans reversed. Put a lute in her hands and let her sing and the power is strengthened: her lover finds himself transported to the worlds she sings about; her capturer finds himself falling in love. Even so, the purest manifestation of this power is in the written word. On at least two occasions, her tormentors make the mistake of giving her brush and paper by way of mocking her: but in so doing they unleash her mesmerizing power. The judge annuls the sentence he was about to pronounce; her lover's father, who has just had her arrested, is converted to a loyal ally; the vengeful woman who trapped her is forced to reconsider her plans.

Her siblings, however, are immune to the superhuman force of Kiều's literary gift. A prophet is never recognized in his own country, nor a poet in hers, and so it is for Kiều. She carves on the tree above Đạm Tiên's grave not one but two poems, the first of which is powerful enough literally to awaken the dead, and yet Vân and Quan remain unmoved. They poke fun at their sister for taking herself – and life – too seriously. Nguyễn Du's message is also his medium, using fluid, startling language to bring Kiều's story to life, using the redemptive power of poetry to resolve the seemingly intractable contradictions of his own life. In the final scene of the poem, Kiều renounces her art, hanging up her lute so that the song for Kim becomes her final lament. This woman who has lived life so fully is now ready to relinquish its material pleasures.

The Song of Kiều is unequivocally a proto-feminist work. Kiều's impassioned speeches in the opening pages make an explicit connection between Đạm Tiên's suffering and the suffering of all women; foreseeing her own tragic end, she links that also with the lot of women in general. Given the crushingly patriarchal nature of dynastic empires in both Vietnam and China, it is remarkable that women should play such prominent roles in every episode of the poem. Kiều drives the plot, of course, and there are always women around to comfort or support her, and yet women count among the story's most memorable villains too: the brothel-keepers, the vindictive wife. Yet it is sisterly solidarity that enables Kiều to forgive Lady Hoạn, who has done her such harm.

Another feature that gives *The Song of Kiều* a surprisingly modern feel is the cinematic quality of its imagery. This linguistic concision is a feature of other East Asian literatures also: we might think of the haiku of Japan, or of those translations of Chinese poetry that inspired imagists to re-energize the Western concept of modern poetry. In *Kiều*, this manifests itself in the precise epiphanies that punctuate the action at key moments. To take one example, when Kim first breaks the bad news to Kiều that he has to leave her, the next lines read like a montage of atmospheric images: 'The fields are strange in the dawn light. / Cuckoos call sadly from thickets. / Wild geese take flight at the sky's edge . . .' Or another, after Kiều escapes from the temple, the poem cuts to: 'Mist swirls across the sand, towards a wooded hill. / Cocks crow from moonlit huts; she presses / fresh shoeprints onto a dew-soaked bridge.' There are many such examples.

Certain visual motifs provide structure and cohesion to the narrative. One of the most frequent motifs is of running water, from the pretty brook in the opening scene, through the regular dripping and trickling of the rain, to the mighty Qiantang river itself, the setting for the dramatic climax predicted by both Đạm Tiên and Tam Hợp. Kiều's suicide attempt is thus foreshadowed throughout the poem, not least by her own early understanding of herself as 'a petal on flowing water, a water fern / catching and drifting along a swollen stream'.

We should not let Kiều's apparent fatalism deceive us, though, for she is a very unreliable proclaimer of her own helplessness. At every step of the way, it is Kiều who makes the key decisions that alter the course of her life, even as she waxes lyrical about being a raindrop that does not know whether it is heading for a farmer's field or a palace garden.

The landscape of *Kiều* is a fictional one with roots in a particular *wokou*–Ming conflict, and yet it is so far removed from that reality that it becomes first Vietnamese and then universal. The poet-diplomat who found himself miserably trapped by the vicelike grip of contemporary politics, of dynastic shifts that crush ordinary people in the grinding of their gears, devised for himself an escape route in the form of Kiều and the transcendence of her lyrical gift. This is the myth that has fortified the ordinary people of Vietnam throughout the repeated conflicts which the twentieth century threw at them, and that will sustain them throughout the current century and beyond. It is a myth that we are also invited to share, holding out the hope that innocence and honesty and poetry and song will not only survive, but will forever outlive, the myopic cruelty of the momentarily powerful.

NOTES

1.   Huỳnh Sanh Thông (1983:xi)
2.   My complete version of Hồ Chí Minh's Prison Diaries was published by Modern Poetry in Translation (Series 3, No. 15) in *Poetry and the State* (2011), and further anthologised in *Centres of Cataclysm* (2016: Bloodaxe Books).
3.   Founded in 1957, Thế Giới (literally 'world' or 'universe') is Vietnam's state-run foreign publishing house.
4.   When Keats first looked into Chapman's Homer, he would have expected to find *The Iliad* and *The Odyssey* inside, albeit more vigorously expressed than in Pope or Dryden. The Spanish explorers, by contrast, would have had no idea what they were going to find on the other side of that peak in Darien. For many Western readers, opening *Kiều* for the first time is like discovering a whole new subcontinent that we barely knew existed.
5.   In a 2015 interview on Vietnamese television, the American scholar Charles Benoit spoke about this usefulness of knowing *Kiều*: 'If I was living in Vietnam, it meant that I could always have something to talk about to people who were at this level (*gestures high*) or this level (*gestures low*). It didn't matter. There was always something I could talk about that was *their* topic, not my topic. Many times, Vietnamese talk to foreigners about whatever foreigners are interested in. But this was something I could talk about, [that] I could predict that Vietnamese would be [interested in], so it was easy to have conversations.'

6.   Literally 'six-eight' verse, *lục bát* is a demotic Vietnamese form that alternates lines of six and eight syllables, interwoven by a rigorous internal and external rhyme scheme. A popular form used for ballads as well as more literary works, *lục bát* for the Vietnamese is what terza rima is for the Italians, or iambic pentameter for the English.

7.   Of course, it is much shorter than either of those works, coming in at just 3,254 lines, compared with more than 10,000 for Milton's work and more than 14,000 for Dante's.

8.   See, for example, *Minh Hoa Kiều*, a musical collaboration between the songwriter Phạm Duy (1921–2013) and his son Duy Cường, published in a series of three CDs (1997, 2001 and 2005).

9.   Two such readers would be the East Asian specialists Eric Henry and Charles Benoit, each of whom has independently carried out extensive research into the primary sources of *Kiều*.

10. The Chinese term *wokou* (倭寇) literally means 'dwarf pirates' or 'Japanese bandits', and the earliest *wokou* had indeed operated from islands off the coast of Japan. By the middle 1500s, however, most of these *wokou* were neither dwarves nor Japanese, but local Chinese from the southern provinces; not only that, but many of them would have been willing to abandon piracy and banditry if the Ming had made it possible for them to trade legally.

11. The name can be translated as 'Pure-Hearted Talented Man'.

12. In translating from Chinese to Vietnamese, *Jīn* becomes *Kim*, *Yún* becomes *Vân* and *Qiáo* becomes *Kiều*. *Zhuàn* (meaning 'story' or 'biography') becomes *Truyện* in Vietnamese.

13. Eric Henry (1976/1982:6) explains that the undated original manuscript of *Jīn Yún Qiáo Zhuàn* is part of a group of fifteen talent-beauty novels collected by the 'Master of Tian Hua Library'. Only three of these books are dated – the earliest being 1658 and the latest two being 1672. This circumstantial evidence alone suggests a date for *Jīn Yún Qiáo Zhuàn* in the second half of the seventeenth century.

14. The Six Classics (in chronological order, from the fourteenth to the eighteenth centuries) are: *Shuihu Zhuan* (*Water Margin*, 水滸傳); *Sanguo Yanyi* (*Romance of the Three Kingdoms*, 三國演義); *Xi You Ji* (*Journey to the West*, 西遊記); *Jin Ping Mei* (*The Plum in the Golden Vase*, 金瓶梅); *Hong Lou Meng* (*Dream of the Red Chamber*, 紅樓夢); and *Rulin Waishi* (*The Scholars*, 儒林外史).

15. *Haoqiu Zhuan* (*The Pleasing History*, 好逑傳), translated by Thomas Percy and James Wilkinson, was published in English in 1761, with later translations into German (1766) and French (1842); *Yu Jiao Li* (*Les Deux*

Cousines, 玉嬌梨) translated by Jean-Pierre Abel-Rémusat, was published in French in 1826; *Ping Shan Leng Yan* (*Les Deux Jeunes Filles Lettrées*, 平山冷燕), translated by Stanislas Julien, followed in 1860. By contrast, the first European attempt at a translation of one of the Chinese classics was made by the British Vice-Consul in Macao, Henry Bencraft Joly (1857–98) as a kind of self-study exercise to improve his Chinese. He published his version of *Hong Lou Meng* (紅樓夢) as *The Dream of the Red Chamber* in 1892. It can be accessed at Project Gutenberg here: < http://www.gutenberg.org/cache/epub/9603/pg9603-images. html>

16.   Tolstoy's *War and Peace* (1869), for example.

17.   This kind of polygamous arrangement was not unusual in Ming-era literature. *A Song of Five Phoenixes* (五鳳吟) tells the tender love story between one man and five women (two ladies and their three chambermaids), and recounts the touching tale of how he is first separated from them and then happily reunited with them. See Eric Henry (1976/1982:10).

18.   Huỳnh Sanh Thông (1983:202).

19.   Eric Henry (1976/82:3).

20.   This means that Kiều, as the eldest of three adolescent siblings, is perhaps in her very late teens at the start of the story, and is in her early to mid-thirties by the end of it.

21.   The other non-Chinese dynasties to rule China were both ruled by the people best known today as the Manchu (formerly the Jurchen), a semi-nomadic people originally located between China and Korea who founded both the Great Jin (1115–1234) and Qing (1644–1912) dynasties.

22.   Marco Polo was a convict in a Genoese jail in 1298 when he told his travel stories to a fellow prisoner, Rustichello of Pisa, who happened to have literary connections and a talent for storytelling. At the time they were both unaware that Kublai Khan had died four years earlier. The cause of Polo's imprisonment was that he had been a ship's captain in the Venetian navy that had been annihilated by the Genoese at the Battle of Curzola (1298).

23.   Writing *Africa*, in the early 1340s, Petrarch would express that feeling of living in the Dark Ages in essentially those terms.

24.   Khanbalik's interim name change was originally to 'Beiping' (northern peace) before the yin-yang notion of dual capitals was settled upon.

25.   The term 'Ming' has several other associations. To give three examples: (1) It forms part of the Chinese term given to Manichaeism (*Ming Jiao*), which since the Tang dynasty had been a proscribed

clandestine religion. Manichaeism (founded by the Persian prophet Mani) is based on the idea that goodness (light) is forever struggling to overcome evil (darkness). (Manichaeism also permeates European notions of their own 'Dark Ages' – see note 23.) In his struggle to oust the Yuan, Zhu Yuanzhang had first to defeat a rival rebel faction that was predominantly Manichaean. His choice of the name 'Ming' was partly intended to keep the survivors of that defeated group on board. (2) Fiery brightness is also considered to be yang (陽), contrasted with the yin (陰) of water. The south is considered yang while the north is yin. By choosing a pair of capitals, the Ming were seeking to affirm a yin-yang balance; by choosing the name 'Ming', they were giving primacy to the south – a primacy that during the course of the dynasty would shift steadily northwards. (3) In Vietnamese, the same ideogram is transliterated 'minh', as in Hồ Chí Minh ('Ho of the bright spirits', a pseudonym he chose for himself) and his political party, the Việt Minh ('bright people').

26. By contrast, speakers whose languages share the same alphabet can pronounce letters in a similar way, but they will understand quite different meanings. For example, English and Spanish speakers will look at the three symbols 'pan' and pronounce them more or less the same, although the first group is thinking of a cooking utensil and the second of a loaf of bread.

27. Of course, this no longer applies to Vietnam, which after the First World War switched to an alphabetic script. Korea developed its own script in the 1440s in order to promote literacy, and yet traces of its Chinese origins remain in modern Korea. The ideogram 日, for example, which is pronounced rì in Chinese and nhật in Vietnamese, is pronounced il in Korean, as in the name of the former President of North Korea, Kim Jong Il. The meaning is 'sun' in all three languages. The Vietnamese term for Sunday, devised by Portuguese Catholic missionaries in the seventeenth century, is chủ nhật (originally written as 主日), whose literal meaning is 'main sun', with 'sun' having the obvious connotation of 'a day'.

28. These were heavily patriarchal societies and positions of authority were almost exclusively held by men, Empress Wu Zetian (624–705) notwithstanding.

29. Certain Chinese proverbs refer to this tendency for the children of the rich to squander the family wealth: 'Wealth does not last beyond three generations' (富不過三代), for example, or 'Keeping it is harder than getting it' (創業易,守成難). The term fu er dai (富二代) is a derogatory term for young people born into rich families.

30. The very existence of modern Shanghai bears witness to the extremely restrictive effect of the centuries-long Ming/Qing sea ban. The events that laid the groundwork for *The Song of Kiều* took place in what is now the hinterland of Shanghai – Hu Zongxian's ambush of Xu Hai, for example, took place at Shenzhuang (沈庄) near Zhapu (乍浦), which is currently a small satellite town a couple of hours' drive from the city centre – and yet 'Shanghai' was at that time an insignificant fishing village, so tiny that it is never mentioned in any of the historical or fictional accounts of those events. When China finally opened up to international trade, in the middle of the nineteenth century, this triggered a population explosion so powerful that the little fishing village became what it is today – arguably the largest city in the world, with a population exceeding 24 million.

31. Most of these details come from the account written by Johann Adam Schall von Bell (1591–1666), a German-born Jesuit who lived in the Forbidden City and is known in Chinese as Tang Ruowang (湯若望). Like Jin Shengtan, he also found himself imprisoned in the anti-intellectual purge that followed the death of the Shunzhi emperor, the context in which *Jīn Yún Qiáo Zhuàn* was first published.

32. He refers to other critics as fools (傖, *cang*) throughout.

33. None of this did the Suzhou magistrate any good – he lost his post a few months later and was executed in Nanjing the following year.

34. 清風不識字, 何故亂翻書.

35. The Shunzhi emperor's support for the arts should not be overstated, however – in 1660 he condemned Zhang Jinyan (張晋彥) to death after interpreting a sentence in one of his books as treasonable.

36. 'Why then must the slick and banal novels be studied?' writes Eric Henry. 'They must be studied because they are profoundly different from the great novels; so different that any literary historian who ignores them will have mistaken ideas concerning Chinese literature' (1976/82:5).

37. This may remind us of Bai T. Moore's *Murder in the Cassava Patch* (1968), familiar to almost every Liberian and yet virtually unknown outside the country; readers who know it well are often surprised to find that it is based on a real murder that took place in 1959. Similarly, many readers of Nabokov's *Lolita* (1955) have been surprised to learn in recent years of that novel's roots in the 1948 abduction of Sally Horner. See Sarah Weinman's *The Real Lolita*, for example (London: Weidenfeld & Nicolson, 2018).

38. Yan Song eventually fell out of favour and died, disgraced and demented, in 1567. He is recorded in the official Ming history as one of the

dynasty's six most treacherous ministers. A Chinese opera about his life (*Beating Yan Song*, 打嚴嵩) was produced in the late nineteenth century, telling of a talented scholar who was loyal to his parents but whose two-faced flattery of the emperor proved his undoing. It remains a popular classic.

39. The Ming official and the pirate chief both came from the south of what is now Anhui province. Hu Zongxian was from Kengkou, Xuancheng district; Wang Zhi was from neighbouring Huangshan.

40. A translation of this account appears in the Appendix (p. 153).

41. There are other antecedents also – Huỳnh Sanh Thông, for example, notes that Nguyễn Du's physical description of Từ Hải, comparing him both to a tiger and a swallow, mirrors the description traditionally accorded to Ban Chao (32–102 CE), an explorer and military general of the Eastern Han dynasty.

42. The phrase is taken from a 1774 letter from a Spanish Franciscan missionary, Diego de Jumilla, describing how local peasants viewed the uprising (cited in Dutton 2006:41).

43. Nguyễn is currently second only to Smith as the commonest surname in Melbourne, for example, and is the fifty-sixth most popular surname in the whole of Norway. The most common surname in Great Britain, Smith, is shared by a little over 1 per cent of the population, with a similar percentage for the name Murphy in Ireland. In both cases, the surname has been boosted by travelling communities choosing a common surname they had heard locally (i.e. Smith in Britain and Murphy in Ireland). Something similar happened – but on an exponential scale – to the name Nguyễn in Vietnam.

44. They were eventually demoted by the French occupation which followed the treaty of 1862.

45. Deborah Wong (2004:110).

Further Reading

Benoit, Charles, 'The evolution of the Wang Cuiqiao tale: from historical event in China to literary masterpiece in Việt Nam', Harvard (PhD thesis, 1981)

Dutton, George, *The Tây Sơn Uprising: Society and Rebellion in Eighteenth-Century Vietnam* (Honolulu: University of Hawai'i Press, 2006)

Fairbank, John K. (ed.), *The Cambridge History of China*, Volume 10: *Late Ch'ing, 1800–1911, Part 1* (Cambridge: Cambridge University Press, 1978)

Fairbank, John K. and Kwang-Ching Liu (eds), *The Cambridge History of China*, Volume 11: *Late Ch'ing, 1800–1911, Part 2* (Cambridge: Cambridge University Press, 1980)

Fletcher, Joseph, 'Sino-Russian relations, 1800–62', in *The Cambridge History of China*, Volume 10: John K. Fairbank (ed.), *Late Ch'ing, 1800–1911, Part 1* (Cambridge: Cambridge University Press, 1978), Chapter 7

Geiss, James, 'The Cheng-te reign, 1506–1521', in *The Cambridge History of China*, Volume 7: Frederick W. Mote and Denis Twitchett (eds), *The Ming Dynasty 1368–1644, Part 1* (Cambridge: Cambridge University Press, 1988), Chapter 7

Geiss, James, 'The Chia-ching reign, 1522–1566', in Mote and Twitchett (eds), *The Ming Dynasty 1368–1644, Part 1*, Chapter 8

Hao, Yen-p'ing and Erh-min Wang, 'Changing Chinese views of Western relations, 1840–95', in John K. Fairbank and Kwang-Ching Liu (eds), *The Cambridge History of China*, Volume 11: *Late Ch'ing, 1800–1911, Part 2* (Cambridge: Cambridge University Press, 1980)

Henry, Eric, 'On the nature, structure and evolution of Jīn Yún Qiáo Zhuàn', Dartmouth College (unpublished MPhil dissertation, 1976, revised 1982)

Hucker, Charles O., 'Hu Tsung-hsien's Campaign against Hsü Hai, 1556', in *Chinese Ways in Warfare*, ed. Frank A. Kierman, Jr, and John K. Fairbank (Cambridge, MA: Harvard University Press, 1974), pp. 273–307

Hummel, Arthur W. (ed.), *Eminent Chinese of the Ch'ing Period (1644–1912) Volume I (A–O)* (Washington, DC: United States Government Printing Office, 1943)

Ma, Ning, 'The Saintly Prostitute in *Jīn Yún Qiáo Zhuàn*', Princeton University (pp 123–132 of unpublished PhD thesis, 2008)

Mote, Frederick W. and Denis Twitchett (eds), *The Cambridge History of China*, Volume 7: *The Ming Dynasty, 1368–1644, Part 1* (Cambridge: Cambridge University Press, 1988)

Nguyen, Viet Thanh, *Nothing Ever Dies: Vietnam and the Memory of War* (Cambridge, MA: Harvard University Press, 2016)

Peterson, Willard J. (ed.), *The Cambridge History of China*, Volume 9, Part One: *The Ch'ing Empire to 1800* (Cambridge: Cambridge University Press, 2002)

Turnbull, Stephen, *Pirate of the Far East: 811–1639* (Oxford: Osprey, 2012)

Twitchett, Denis and Frederick W. Mote (eds), *The Cambridge History of China*, Volume 8: *The Ming Dynasty, 1368–1644, Part 2* (Cambridge: Cambridge University Press, 1998)

Wong, Deborah, *Speak it Louder: Asian Americans Making Music* (London: Routledge, 2004)

Wong Sin Kiong (ed.), *Confucianism, Chinese History and Society* (Singapore: World Scientific, 2012)

Other versions of *Kiều* in English
(in chronological order of publication)

Lê-Xuân-Thủy (ed. and trans.), *Nguyễn Du: Kim Vân Kiều* (Saigon, 1963; reprinted by Silk Pagoda, 2006). A revised and versified edition was published as *The Soul of Poetry inside Kim Vân Kiều* (Bloomington, IN: Author House, 2010)

Huỳnh Sanh Thông (ed. and trans.), *Nguyễn Du: The Tale of Kiều: A Bilingual Edition of Truyện Kiều* (New Haven, CT: Yale University Press, 1983)

Michael Counsell (trans.), *Nguyễn Du: Kiều* (Hanoi: Thế Giới, 1994)

Vladislav Zhukov (trans.), *The Kim Vân Kieu of Nguyen Du (1765–1820)* (Canberra: Pandanus Books, 2004)

Arno Abbey (trans.), *Nguyen Du: Kieu: An English Version Adapted from Nguyen Khac Vien's French Translation* (Bloomington, IN: AuthorHouse, 2008)

Charles Benoit has for many years been working on a definitive edition of *Truyện Kiều*, which he is aiming to complete by 2020, to mark the 200th anniversary of Nguyễn Du's death. Based on the five extant *nôm* editions of *Đoạn Trường Tân Thanh* (1866, 1870, 1871, 1872 and 1902), this thoroughly annotated version is designed to function as an online edition, presenting the original text both in *chữ Nôm* and in *Quốc ngữ* script, alongside Benoit's English translation, allowing Anglophone readers to access a literal word-by-word translation and explanatory notes by clicking on each character.

WEB ADDRESSES

The interview with Charles Benoit (referenced in note 4 of the Introduction) can be accessed at <http://english.vtv.vn/news/the-tale-of-kieu-in-the-heart-of-international-friends-20151125172946114.htm>

The original text of the poem (in *Quốc ngữ* script) can be accessed at <http://www.informatik.uni-leipzig.de/~duc/sach/kieu/index.html>

The map opposite illustrates a sometimes overlooked feature of *The Song of Kiều*, namely that the characters' journeys cover a vast area, figuratively re-knitting together a divided nation. The tranquillity of the opening scenes is disrupted when Kim is called away to Liaoyang, which was not only the former capital of the Jurchen Jin dynasty (1115–1234) but also provided the base from which the Manchu launched their first offensive against the Ming (1621–5). Kiều herself is from the northern capital, Beijing. She heads first to Linzi, originally the capital of the state of Qi (323–221 BCE); Qin Shi Huang's capture of Linzi famously completed the original unification of China. Kiều spends the middle section of the story in Wuxi, then at the epicentre of China's traditionally most trade-oriented region. At the time *Jīn Yún Qiáo Zhuàn* was published, that region formed the heartland of Southern Ming resistance against the Qing. Kiều's final brothel, where she meets Từ Hải, is in Tiantai, the founding location of the most important branch of Chinese Buddhism. Từ Hải himself comes from Guangdong in the far south, where currently we would find Hong Kong.

Five Journeys in *The Song of Kiều*

N

MONGOLIA

MANCHURIA

the Great
Wall

① Liaoyang

Beijing

② Linzi

Linqing

CHINA

③

Nanjing

④

KOREA

JAPAN

Wuxi

Hangzhou ⑤ Ningbo

Qiantang R.

Tiantai

CHINA

VIETNAM

Guangdong

VIETNAM

| 0 | 300 miles |
| 0 | 600 kms |

① Kim's journey to collect his uncle's corpse
② Kiều's first journey to Linzi
③ Thúc travels overland to Linzi
④ Kiều is abducted to Wuxi by sea
⑤ Kiều travels to the Bạc brothel

The Tây Sơn brothers, during their short-lived dynasty, divided Vietnam between them as illustrated on the facing page. The middle brother, Nguyễn Huệ, took control of the whole northern region, while his elder brother, Nguyễn Nhạc, ruled over the midland area that had originally been the brothers' homeland, and Nguyễn Lữ ruled over the south, where today we would find Hồ Chí Minh City (Saigon). Note that Nguyễn Huệ's territory includes both the Trịnh capital in modern-day Hanoi and also the Nguyễn capital in modern-day Huế.

The map also shows some key events in the life of Nguyễn Du, a northerner whose writings suggest some sympathy for the Tây Sơn rebellion, which he and his family officially opposed. It was during his 1813 mission to the Qing court in Beijing that Du first came across a copy of *Jīn Yún Qiáo Zhuàn*, reworking it into *The Song of Kiều*.

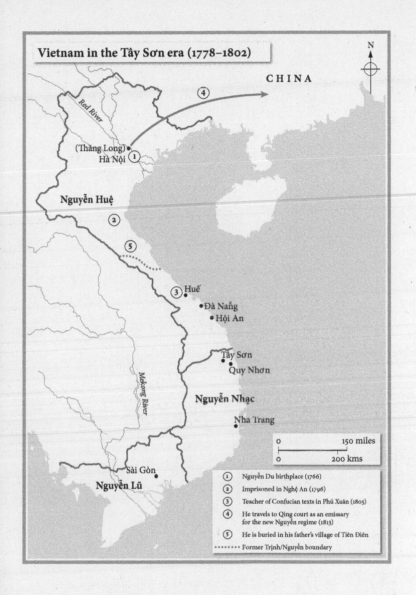

Vietnam in the Tây Sơn era (1778–1802)

N

CHINA

Red River

④

(Thăng Long) ①
Hà Nội

Nguyễn Huệ

②

⑤

③ Huế
● Đà Nẵng
● Hội An

Tây Sơn
● Quy Nhơn

Nguyễn Nhạc

● Nha Trang

Mekong River

0   150 miles

0   200 kms

● Sài Gòn

Nguyễn Lữ

① Nguyễn Du birthplace (1766)

② Imprisoned in Nghệ An (1796)

③ Teacher of Confucian texts in Phú Xuân (1805)

④ He travels to Qing court as an emissary
  for the new Nguyễn regime (1813)

⑤ He is buried in his father's village of Tiên Điền

••••••• Former Trịnh/Nguyễn boundary

THE SONG OF KIỀU

A NEW LAMENT

một

mót: desire, to glean
mọt: wormhole
mốt: fashion, trend
một: one

1

It's an old story: good luck and good looks
don't always mix.
Tragedy is circular and infinite.
The plain never believe it,
but good-looking people meet with hard times too.

It's true.
Our ending is inevitable:
long years betray the beautiful.[1]

This manuscript is ancient, priceless,
bamboo-rolled, perfumed with musty spices.
Sit comfortably by this good light, that you may learn
the hard-won lesson that these characters contain.

*

In the middle of the Ming dynasty, Jiajing is on the throne.
Both capitals are peaceful.[2] A poor mandarin
named Vương has three children:
a handsome son, Vương Quan,
and two daughters, Kiều and Vân.

The sisters are slender as saplings and lovely
as snow fresh fallen from a winter sky.
The gentle glow of a full moon
might remind you of the round face of Vân.
Her words sparkle, precious as jewels,
and her smile is as soft as rose petals.

But Kiều is still more beautiful. Her eyes
are dark and troubled as November seas.
Spring flowers envy her grave beauty

and the mountain ash shivers with jealousy
whenever she passes by.
Her smile flashes like a thunderbolt.
A fine painter, singer and poet,
she makes mournful melodies on her lute:
the saddest and the sweetest is 'Cruel Fate'.

Young men buzz beyond the outer wall:
bees among the honeysuckle.

Swallows and spring days fly like shuttles
over green lawns splashed with white petals
from the branches of the pear trees.

It is April, the Feast of Pure Light,[3] when families
visit the graves of their ancestors: pulling weeds
and burning incense. Like orioles or swifts,
people flit about. The sisters and their brother dress up
and step outside.

Bright men and lovely women crowd
the streets:[4] wave upon wave of fashionable clothes,
slowing the flow of carriages and horses.
Everywhere, little hills and mounds are strewn
with paper coins, fake gold and smouldering incense.

The sun sets, the shadows lengthen,
and the sisters and their brother turn for home.
Strolling hand-in-hand beside a pretty brook,
they remark its gentle beauty. They pause to look.

Downstream, beside a little bridge,
they notice a tomb mottled by mushrooms
and rotten greenish-yellow weeds.

Kiều asks: 'On this bright day when we respect the dead,
why has this grave alone been left untended?'

'I can answer that,' her brother replies.
'Beneath that dappled stone a bright truth lies.
Her name was Đạm Tiên. Once she sang
more joyfully than skylarks, and her song
brought swifts and orioles to her door.
But roses are fragile: one crisp spring day, she died.

'That same morning, a ship sailed into port.
On board was a stranger who had heard
of her beautiful voice; he had planned
to woo and win her in her own homeland.
But the hairpin was snapped, the vase was smashed
and the silence of death now stilled her room.
The hoof-prints were muddied, the wheel-ruts overgrown.

'The young man wept from wordless grief.
He could no longer meet the girl he had dreamed of:
cruel fate had kept them apart.
He vowed no other would ever hold his heart.

'He placed Đạm Tiên on a length of catalpa, laid her
in a beaded carriage, and buried her just here
beneath the dirt and dust and grass and flowers.
But the moon-hare dips and the sun-crow dives
and weeds grow thick on forgotten graves.'

Kiều now brims with a strange melancholy
till tiny pearls run down her cheeks.

'A woman's world is weaved from woe,' she says,
'and the only thing we dream of is despair.
God rips off our wings. God makes us die.
Đạm Tiên, once a wished-for wife,

is now a bony basket of wormy earth.
Those boys are gone that used to hold her,
and the promises they made are fallen to silence.
Since no one is left to mourn for her,
I will burn these few sticks of incense
to mark how we have chanced upon her grave.
Perhaps she can see us, from her Yellow Springs.'[5]

Then Kiều murmurs a heartfelt prayer
and stoops to lay some grass upon the spot.
Twilight falls across the rotting weeds
and an evening breeze rustles the barley reeds.
She draws a pin from her hair and carves
a perfect four-line poem on a nearby tree.
She steps back. She clears her mind,
then melts into tears, like a squall of sudden rain.
She pictures herself alone on a dark night,
where shapeless horrors crowd the road ahead.
She is a petal on flowing water, a water fern
catching and drifting along a swollen stream.

Vân laughs and says: 'My sister, how silly you are
to waste hot tears on a long-dead stranger.'

Kiều answers: 'But since this earth began,
cruel fate has cursed all women.
I look on Đạm Tiên's mossy tomb,
and see my own, in days to come.'

Quan says: 'So this is the real story.
You talk of Đạm Tiên, but weep for yourself.
Look, it's getting dark. There is a chill in the air,
and we still have a long walk home.'

'When stars die, their fire is gone,'
says Kiều, 'but a dwindling light shines on.
My soul has found its mate in this gloomy place.
Let's wait a while. I want to meet her ghost.'

Before they can answer, a tornado swirls up.
It shakes the tree and tears off its leaves,
trailing a strange perfume in its wake.
They look along the path that the wind took
to find it left damp footprints on the moss.

Vân and Quan stare at each other, dumbfounded.

Kiều says: 'See the fierce power of a poem.
Learn how words can leap across the years.
She is my sister, though I am alive and she is dead.'

Again she takes the pin from her hair
and adds a verse of thanks to Đạm Tiên.
This one is a word picture in the old style,
free from the shackles of rhyme and metre.

And while she makes that fresh mark on the bark,
the others hear a tinkle of harness bells.

A young man is riding a snow-white colt,
holding the reins loose. Across his shoulder
is a bag stuffed with wind and moonlight,
which is what the world calls poetry.
Behind him, two small boys skip to keep up.
His coat is grass-green and sky-blue.

He calls a brisk hello and dismounts,
leading the frisky colt in their direction.
Through the dusk, his slippered feet
sparkle like rubies and polished jasper.

Quan goes to greet him – it's his classmate from school –
but the girls step to one side.

The sisters already know Trọng Kim by sight:
a handsome, polite and honey-tongued young man.
His family owns a decent bit of land.

He knows them too. How well he knows these girls!
Hidden in their father's tidy house,
they might as well have lived across a dozen rivers;
but he has crossed those valleys in his dreams.[6]
Today, the Feast of Light, when we tell our futures
from the budding of the leaves,
his wanderings have brought him to these orchids.
He admires them both. He thinks: red shadows[7]
are beautiful in both spring and autumn.

When bright young boys encounter lovely girls,
their mouths may be silent but their hearts run wild.
They live in that dangerous country
where the waking world meets dreams.

It is getting dark.
The girls watch Kim as he turns and walks away.
The clear stream flows under the bridge.
The willow trails silky fingers through its twilit waters.

*

Kiều goes home. She draws the flowered blinds.
The night gong has sounded.
The moon peeps through the window,
spilling silver pools across the courtyard,
marking out the silhouettes of trees.
A red camellia bends towards the east:
dewdrops trickle and fall.

Alone in silence, Kiểu gazes at the shadowy moon,
thinking of what has been and what is yet to come:

'Each of us must lie in an unkempt grave.
Our bright and sparkling life is a fragile bubble.
And that fine young man, who came across my path.
Has fate dreamed up some plan for him and me?'

Seared with these burning thoughts, she writes
a new lyric charged with everything she feels.
Moonlight slants diagonals through the blinds.
She rests her head against the window frame.

Suddenly a girl, wet with rain,
dressed with snow,
appears in the dusky air.
Her feet float on lotus blooms.

Kiểu starts awake. She greets her:
'Who are you? Have you come from the lost world
where peach trees always bloom beside a fairy stream?'

'I am your sister soul,' the other says.
'Have you forgotten? We met today!
My lonely bed lies out there, to the west,
beside a brook that runs beneath a bridge.
You pitied me, you carved a poem on that tree
whose roots run through my head.

'I brought your work to my chief:
the head of the Company of Sadness,
of all those who are doomed
to live and die with a broken heart.[8]
He told me your name belongs with ours.
We ride in the same boat.
But the skipper liked your poem.

He gave me ten new titles
and asked if you will weave once more
your magic with a brush.'

Kiều seizes a brush and dashes off ten poems
in a single flow of movement and idea.

Đạm Tiên takes up the paper and exclaims:
'How wonderfully these words are worked!
We'll put them in the Book of Songs of Sadness.
They will take pride of place.'

The visitor turns to leave. Kiều reaches out a hand
to grasp her ghostly gown.

A sudden gust of wind rattles the blinds.
She wakes. She realizes that she must have dreamed.
She looks around, but nowhere sees the girl,
yet still can sense her perfume in the air.

Alone with her thoughts in the black night,
Kiều stares into the long road ahead.
She is a floating petal on a swollen stream.
She is a broken fern in a swift current
and she weeps because she knows that fate is cruel.

Her sobbing awakes her gentle mother
on the other side of the phoenix drapes.

'What's wrong? Why are you crying
in the middle of this night?
Your cheeks are pear blossoms
drenched with rain.'

'Mother, you bore me and you brought me up,
while I have given you nothing in return.
Today, the three of us found Đạm Tiên's grave.
That singer came to see me in my dream.
She told me that my fate is sealed for sorrow,
and bade me write ten songs, which I've just done.
Read them. See what meaning they contain.
Now I know my life will have no happy ending.'

Her mother strokes her hair and says,
'Hush, child – there are worse things in the world
than dreams and ghosts.'

Kiều calms a little. But once her mother leaves,
she falls again to soundless tears.
Outside her window, an oriole sings.
A catkin drops into a neighbour's yard.
Moonlight slopes through the eaves.
Kiều is left to solitude and silence.

*

People in love are foolish creatures.
They have strange habits.
When Kim goes home to his book-lined walls,
he realizes that he has fallen in love with Kiều.
Hers is the face he sees before he sleeps.
She is the one who finds him in his dreams.
Each day away from her he calls three autumns.

Silk curtains hide her distant windows:
he wants to open them, to touch the rose within.
The moon is always waning, the lamp is burning low:
he longs to press his face against her face.
In his room, the air is frosty, copper-cold:
his brushes dry; his lute strings hanging loose.

Bamboo blinds rattle in the wind.
Incense stirs his desire.
This tea tastes dull:
it lacks the lick of her lips.

If fate had not meant to draw us together,
then why did she suddenly appear, that evening,
with her beauty that can topple city walls,
to dazzle and enthral me with her smile?

He returns to the graveside, where first he found the girl.
It is the turn of a brook, like any other:
lush green grass and clear water.
Sadness hangs on the breeze at dusk.
The thin reeds sway, mocking him.
He can think of nothing else, except her.

He keeps walking, till he reaches her Blue Bridge.
The gate is locked, the wall is high.
He wonders how he might get in.

For instance, he could write a poem,
so seductive, so well made, it will win her heart,
on the underside of a fallen leaf,
and he will set that red leaf on a little stream
that will carry the poem under these stony walls –
but there is no such stream.

Another plan. He writes the same poem
and ties it to the leg of a friendly bluebird,
and persuades the bird to squeeze its feathered form
through a crack in the stonework
to fly to her with messages of love.
Except there is no such crack
and no such bluebird.

A willow pours its silky curtain.
Behind those leaves, a magpie cackles.
Kiều's gate stays locked and bolted.
Where is she?

There must be another way in.
He strolls about those forbidding walls
and finds, around the back, a vacant house
whose owners are away, a sign that says 'For Rent'.

And that is how the painter Kim becomes Kiều's neighbour.
He brings his books, his lute, and settles in.
He has everything he needs: trees and rocks to hide behind.
The name of the house, in gold letters: 'Birdwatchers' Paradise'.
A good name, because there is a beautiful bird
that he certainly hopes to view.[9]
Each day he opens his window, just a fraction,
to peep towards her eastern wall.
But the spring and the grotto are silent.
He cannot even glimpse her red shadow.

Two months come and go.
One warm afternoon, this side of the wall,
he spies her, walking under peach trees.
He puts down his lute and smooths his gown.
But when he gets outside, she is gone,
her perfume still hanging on the breeze.

He rummages about in the grass and finds
a golden hairpin stuck in the bark of a tree.
He thinks: 'So we are fated to meet! Otherwise,
why would this hairpin have fallen into my hands?'

He stays awake all night, admiring the pin
and its aroma of sandalwood.

At dawn, as the mists are clearing,
he sees Kiều searching on the far side of the wall.
He dresses quickly and creeps towards the spot
where she must be, and says aloud:
'Oh, look, I've just found a hairpin.
How will I ever find its owner?'

Kiều calls across the wall to him:
'You found a pin. I found something better.
That golden pin is worth something, it's true.
But what's worth more is an honest heart
whose first thought, on finding a gem,
is to return it to a stranger.'

Kim says: 'On two sides of the same wall,
beneath the same trees, we are not strangers,
we are neighbours. Thanks to your perfume,
I always know where I can find you.
We've met before, and ever since that day
I've dreamed of this moment.
Stay where you are. I want to ask you something.'

He rushes to fetch a few items from his house:
a pair of gold bracelets, a silk scarf, a stepladder.
He sets it by the wall and steps into the sky.
There is no doubt. This is the same girl.
He gazes at her, the sun behind him.
She turns away.

He says: 'That day we met was the luckiest of my life.
Ever since, I have been pining for you.
Look how thin I am. Like an apricot tree.
I can't eat. Every day I hope to find you
and every day I fail. Until today
which is probably a dream.
I spent the first month in heaven,

the second in hell, thinking
I would never see you again.
But now you are here. And now I ask my question:
Bright mirror, will you shine on this broken fern?'

Kiều thinks for a moment. Then she says:
'My family is poor as ice and pure as snow.
I will love whomever they need me to love.
You speak hot words. They burn me like fire.
But I am my parents' child. I have no right to speak.'

Kim says, 'Today it is windy, tomorrow it might rain.
It's spring. Who knows what will happen next?
I understand your words and they hurt me,
they stab me like a knife.
What good does it do you to hurt me like that?
Just give me a sign that you can love me
and tomorrow I'll speak to the matchmaker.
I have money. Everything will work out fine.
Or give me the opposite sign, and I'm finished.
The potter's wheel will have thrown me off.
It's the end of my pointless life.'

Kiều listens to his lullaby of love:
she likes it, but she fears it too.
She says, 'All these words you tell me are new.
But since I am the one who is hurting you,
I'll stop. I match everything you say.
I will write your words in gold,
I will carve them in stone.'

And this unties the tricky knot that binds his heart.
He gives her the silk scarf and the gold bracelets.
He says, 'One hundred years from now, everything we've said
will still be remembered. Let these little gifts
witness the eternal promise of our love.'

She is holding a sunflower fan.
She gives it to him.
In return, he gives her the gold pin
that had fallen from her hair.
This exchange of gifts unites them for ever
as surely as if they have been pressed together,
fixed firm with lacquer and glue.

Hearing voices from the house behind her,
the two of them flutter like leaves in the wind.
Kim scurries down his ladder and goes home to his books.
Kiều goes back to her bedroom.

*

Stone has tolled with gold: their love deepens,
but their melancholy too.
He might be upstream, she might be down:
they both drink from the same river.

The wall is high that separates them.
Like mist or drifting snows,
they hope to swirl their messages around it.

Windy days, moonlit nights:
petals fade, leaves grow greener.
Spring is coming to an end.

Kiều's maternal grandfather is celebrating his birthday.
Her parents, her brother and sister, prepare a gift.
They put on their finest clothes and set out.
Kiều is left to mind the house.

Alone, with orchids for company,
she covers a table with food for their return.
Then she hurries outside. At the garden wall,
she calls his name softly, through the flowers.
Kim answers the same instant.

He asks her quietly: 'Where have you been? I have waited
so long that my flames were starting to flicker.
Through every lonely night I dreamed of you.
Wait till you see me. My hair is turning grey.'

'Blame the wind and the rain,' she answers.
'That's all that kept me from you.
My family has gone out. Why don't we meet?
We can make up for lost time.'

She skirts the edge of the rockery, to the locked gate
that separates her world from his.
She folds up her sleeves and unlocks it.

She steps into that fabulous country
where peach trees bloom beside a fairy stream.
He looks at her. She looks at him. This is happiness.

She says, 'How kind of you to let me come.'
He answers, 'I hope this changeable weather
is neither too warm nor too cold for you.'

Side by side, they walk towards his studio,
whispering words full of wind and moonlight
that only mountains and rivers can hear.

*

Inkpots, rolled-up poems, a tray for his brushes:
above the desk a watercolour of pine trees.
To Kiều's eyes, Kim's painting seems so finely made
that she can sense the breeze that sways the branches
and feel the snow drip from the needles.

'It's just a little something I dashed off,' says Kim.
'Perhaps if you'd care to add a word or two . . .'

She picks up a brush and puts four lines above the trees,
as if the wind is lashing them with rain.

He marvels at what she has done. 'What a poem!
Neither Ban nor Xie[10] could have matched it.
What kind of saint were you in your previous life
to be blessed with such talent now?'

She says, 'From the first moment I saw you,
I knew that you tread the golden path
towards the emperor's door. You have luck on your side.
But my own dream is fragile as a dragonfly's wing.
The wheel will never spin my fate with yours.
When I was a child, an old man read my face,
and said: "This girl is doomed to blaze like a rocket
and fall as far. That's what happens to poets."
And when I first read your handsome face, I could see
a different road, which leads to luxury.
We don't belong together.'

'That's not true,' says Kim. 'Think how fate
first threw us together. Human beings can fight
to change what heaven has marked out for us.
Our destinies belong to us, not us to them.
And if the knot that binds us falls apart,
I will tie it up again, or die in the attempt.'

They tell each other many secrets of this sort.
Maybe it's their youth, maybe it's the spring wine,
but they talk like this until the sun-crow sets
over the far mountains. Then Kiều remembers
that her family must be coming home, so she hurries away.

*

She finds a message that says the feast is continuing
and her family will not return until much later.
She hangs a silk curtain over the front door.

The garden is now black as night, but Kiều skips into it
and runs across the grass. Moonbeams make shadows
from thick branches. Fireflies shake a sparkling curtain.

The painter has fallen asleep at his desk. He wakes
to hear soft footsteps rushing towards him in the dark.
This must be a dream. He is in that sensual land
where clouds are born from love-making at dusk,
where gentle rain drizzles through the dawn.

'I was drawn to you through the darkness of this night,' says Kiều.
'My path was lit by my love for you.
But now that I have found you,
I think this is only a dream.'

He welcomes her.
He relights the lamps and refills the incense.
Then both of them write messages of love.
With a golden knife, each cuts a lock of hair
which they mingle to form a single cloud.
And throughout that night the moon shines bright
as they make their promises of love.
They whisper little secrets, as tiny as silk threads,
until the word 'FOR EVER' is carved on their bones.

They drink wine out of jade cups.
Their scents intermingle.
They admire each other in the mirror.

Kim says, 'This night is cool and the moon is bright.
Let us make the elixir of life.
Let me pound your magic mortar with my jade pestle.
Or do these words offend you?'

Kiều says, 'I am not offended.
Words are only words. Our promises are made.
But love is not a game.
We should not measure it by how far we have trod,
nor think of battles won, nor places reached.'

Kim says, 'Whatever you wish. But listen.
People tell me you play the lute. You're famous.'
Kiều says, 'My music is nothing. But if you command me,
I have no choice. I have to play.'
He hands her his moon-shaped lute.
Kiều says: 'My little skill
is not worth even the trouble
you took in finding me this lute.'

But she plucks its strings.
She tunes the four strings and the five notes.
And she starts to pluck a rhythm.
What tumbles out is an old song –
'The War between Han and Chu'[11] –
and in the twang of those strings Kim can hear
the clatter of iron and the clash of bronze.
Then she plays Sima's phoenix song,[12]
which won him the heart of Zhuo Wenjun.
It speaks of poetry and forbidden love,
and it aches with ancient sadness.
When she starts Ji Kang's 'Guangling San',[13]

Kim finds himself chasing the shadows of clouds
over dark and troubled seas.
She ends with 'Crossing the Checkpoint',
a song about Wang Zhaojun,[14]
who was married off to a Mongol chief.
In that far country, she longed for home,
echoing the sad song of migrating cranes:
'Here am I. Where are you?'[15]
The whisper of a breeze hides behind the soft notes,
but the harshness falls on Kim like a monsoon.

The lamp flares up, and then it dims.
Kim presses his head against the pillow.
'How beautifully you sing!' he says.
'And yet how terrible are your songs.
Why do you sing of misery? It makes you sad,
and it makes your listeners sad to hear it.'

Kiều says, 'That's the way things are.
Some people are born happy, while others
feel all the tortures that torment us.
I am one of the miserable brigade.
But if you want me to join your happy crew,
I will do my best to change.'

He persuades her. He holds her close
and breathes her rose-like scent.
High waves of lust send him
to a place she would not yet go.

'I told you love is not a game,' she says.
'Hold off your hand and let me speak.
A peach is a tiny fruit. It might seem foolish
to fence a whole orchard to protect so small a prize,
but hear me out. I will be your bride,
and as your bride-to-be I'll live chastely.

There are girls who make love lightly
in the mulberry groves down by the riverbank,
but I am not among them.
Whoever eats a thrown-together dish
misses the loving care of preparation.
Remember those old love stories:
Cui and Zhang[16] were such a beautiful couple
until she gave in to his requests
and the clouds and rain of their passion
wore down the stone and gold of their firm promises.
As they lay, love-spent, limb entwined with limb,
their hearts were already turning to contempt.
They burned out their desire under that western roof
until their young love waned and turned to shame.

'How would it be if I let that happen to us?
Who would be to blame? And why should you rush
to snatch the blossom from the willow?
As long as I live, you must know
that everything I have is yours.'

He hears her speak this common sense.
His admiration grows tenfold.

The moon slants silver beams
through diagonal rafters.

But from nowhere comes a shout,
an urgent cry through the silence of the night –
someone is calling Kim's name.

They start at the sound.

Kiều flies out the back way, to her own house.
Kim hurries through his peach-scented garden
towards the front gate, to answer the midnight call.

hai

hài: curly-toed boots
hái: to pluck
hải: the ocean
hãi: to fear
hại: harmful
hai: two

2

Kim unlocks the brushwood gate. Disaster comes in.
A messenger explains: 'Your uncle is dead
and your father needs you to fetch the corpse
from that far country where the old man died: Liaoyang.'[17]

Kim goes immediately to Kiều's house
to tell her how his uncle's death
must take him far from her embrace.

'No sooner have we met than we must part:
we never even tied love's silky knot.
But look at the moon! It shines on us,
and on our promises of love,
as it will shine for ever.
Though far apart, our hearts will stay together.
Each day away from you will be three winters.
I can never unravel
the twisted chaos of my sorrow.
Take care of yourself, my gold, my jewel,
for you hold the heart of one who must journey far
as the torn and lonely clouds at the end of the sky.'

These words snarl a barbed tangle about her gut.[18]
She stammers and gasps. Then she says:
'How he must hate us, who spins our threads,
who sends us grief before we have known joy.
Let my hair go grey and thin: my love will not.
I will wait for you through the long years,
I will pray for my traveller.
We are promised to each other:
I will never play my lute in another's boat.
Until the mountains crumble and the rivers run dry,
remember me, who spoke these words today.'

They linger, hand in hand. They cannot part.
But the rising sun is now touching the roof beams.
He tries to tear himself away, and fails.
They whisper their goodbyes. They weep.
Step by step he struggles to leave.

Throwing belongings into a knapsack,
he saddles his horse and gallops away.

The fields are strange in the dawn light.
Cuckoos call sadly from thickets.
Wild geese take flight at the sky's edge:
grief for the rider on the long road
who battles with wind and rain,
while his heart grows heavy with love.

*

Kiều stands with her back to the western porch:
her heart is stripped like shredded silk.
She looks through the gate towards the far mists.
She is rose-frail. She is gaunt as a willow.

She is still pacing up and down like this
when her family returns from the birthday feast.

But there is no time even to say hello:
bailiffs were waiting in ambush.
They burst into the house,
swinging clubs and swords. These torturers rush in
with buffalo heads and horse faces.
They hurl a rope about her brother and her father
and lock each of them into a wooden cangue.[19]
These bluebottles buzz dirtily about the house.

They smash workbaskets; they splinter looms;
they grab jewels, money, personal items,
and scoop it all into their greedy sacks.

This attack has come from nowhere:
'What are you doing? What is this all about?'
asks Kiều. The bailiffs answer:
'A silk merchant wants his money back.
Your father owes him a fortune.'

The household is thrown into panic.
The women plead his innocence,
but bailiffs never listen.
The earth trembles and the clouds grow dark,
but they beat away protests with their batons.
They string up Quan and his father by their heels:
dogs would have died of shame at the sight of it.

Their faces wracked with anxiety,
the Vươngs call to heaven for protection.
But bailiffs do what bailiffs do:
bring terror and pain to the innocent,
all for the want of money.

How can Kiều rescue her father?
Poverty gives us such dreadful dilemmas.
If you had to choose between your lover
and your family, how would you decide?

The honest child puts her parents first.
Kiều forgets her promises of love.
'Take your hands off him!' she says.
'If it is money you want, I will give you money.
I will find a husband. Let me settle my father's debts.'

An old bailiff named Zhong is moved by these words:
a bailiff who can feel compassion.
He admires this daughter
and her brave defence of her father.
He cuts down the two prisoners.
He reckons that three hundred liạng
will square the debt and pay off his fellow villains.
Until she finds it, he will lock her father
in the bailiffs' yard – a kind of house arrest.
He gives Kiều three days to find the amount.

And that is how Kiều, still young and naive,
meets the fate that flew in on the wind.
Losing your lover is a little death:
but she who thinks nothing of her own life
cares even less for the loss of love.
She is a raindrop. She does not mind whether she falls
into a mandarin's garden or a farmer's ditch.
She is a blade of young grass that feels grateful
for three months of spring rain.

The matchmakers get wind of her offer
and the story spreads like mist over a field.
An old woman appears at their door, with a man
who intends to ask for Kiều's hand.
She calls him 'Mã, the college graduate'
and says he comes from 'not too far away,
from a district called Linqing'.[20]

Mã is the wrong side of forty, and it shows,
but he is clean-shaven and he wears smart clothes.
He barges in with his servants behind him
and the matchmaker ushers him upstairs.
He takes the best seat without asking,
and waits grandly while they go to fetch Kiều.

She enters the upper room, weighed down
by her father's troubles and her own grief.
With every step, she sheds tears like petals in the breeze:
she trembles like a fawn afraid of the cold rain;
she cannot even face her own reflection in the mirror.
The matchmaker smooths her hair and strokes her hands,
but this makes her feel worse.
She is sad as a chrysanthemum
and thin as an apricot tree.

Mã sizes her up:
he makes her pluck the moon-bowled lute
and tells her to write verses on a fan.
He likes the size and the shape of her.
He says, 'I have come to the Blue Bridge
to find this rare piece of jade.
What's the price of it?'

The matchmaker says, 'Take a look at her:
easily worth one thousand liạng.
But here's the good news. Her family's in trouble.
They will be happy with whatever you pay.'

They talk for hours like this,
until the price of Kiều falls to four hundred liạng.

Once money hits the table,
all canoes paddle smoothly.
Mã and Kiều exchange horoscopes
and fix a date for the wedding.
A message is sent to Zhong,
and old man Vương is allowed to go home.

Imagine the old man as he faces his daughter.
He dies within himself. He says,
'I wanted my child to find a good match.

Why does heaven punish us so?
What liar has ripped my home to pieces?
Bring an axe to break these old bones,
for I cannot face what I have done to my daughter.
Death can visit us only once: let it come for me now.'
He weeps, and bangs his head against the wall.

They hold him back. But he does not calm himself
until his daughter speaks.
Kiều says, 'What is a young girl worth? Nothing
if she does not repay what her parents have done.
Remember Ti Ying,[21] who threw herself at the emperor's feet
to save the life of her father.
Remember Li Ji,[22] who slew the snake dragon
to save her parents from poverty.
A father is a cedar tree: as he grows old
he shoulders many branches.
If you do not let me go, I fear a hurricane
will wreck our family home:
it is better to lose a single flower
and let it scatter in the wind,
in order to be sure that the leaves grow green.
I accept whatever happens to me next.
Think of me as a nipped bud and my leaving
as a necessary pruning.
This is not the time to do something foolish
that will harm yourself and destroy our family.'

The old man is calmed by the wisdom of her words.
They look at one another with tears in their eyes.

Just then, Mã appears at the door
with the bag of silver. They sign the contract.
How strange and cruel is the god of marriage,
linking men to women almost at random!

Money in the hand turns black to white.
At least old man Zhong kept his word:
once the fine was paid, all charges were dismissed.

*

And so the family's troubles are resolved
while they await the wedding day.
Kiều is alone beside the midnight lamp,
her gown damp from her crying.
She twists her hair about her fingers.

She thinks: 'I will accept whatever the future brings.
But I miss my lover, who keeps his vows to me.
How hard he worked to win my heart –
and by winning it, damned himself for ever.
The wine in our cup is not yet dry
with which we toasted our eternal love.
On the road to Liaoyang, Kim cannot suspect
that I have already broken all our vows –
vows that will come to nothing in this life.
In my next life, I would like to be reborn
as a buffalo or a horse, to work for Kim
whose love life is entwined with mine
as bamboo to a plum tree.
But until that day, my crystal heart
must stay below, unmelting,
among the Yellow Springs.'

These secret thoughts spin in circles
as the lamp burns low
and her veil is wet with tears.

Thúy Vân wakes with a start
to find her sister weeping by lamplight.
She says, 'In this great sea change of our life,
it is you who must face our troubles alone.
Is that what keeps you awake tonight?
Or is there some other secret that torments you?'

Kiều says, 'My heart is breaking, for it is caught
in a love net that can never be untangled.
I am nearly ashamed to tell you my secret,
but if I do not speak, I'll bring greater shame
to the one who holds my love.

'I need to ask you a favour. Sit down,
for what I say will change your path for ever.
You remember Kim.
I gave him a fan as token of my love for him.
We drank from the same cup and swore eternal love.
Then from nowhere this storm has come,
forcing me to choose between love and duty.

'You are young, and your spring days are still ahead.
I want you to take my place, in those vows
that only rivers and mountains can hear.
I want you to become Kim's wife.
And though my flesh may have turned to dust,
I will see you, from my Yellow Springs,
and I will smile on your happiness.

'Take these bracelets that he gave me,
and this written vow, and this mingled hair.
Then one day, the two of you can remember
this doomed girl, and keep me in your hearts.
I will be gone. And I have nothing to leave you
except a moon-shaped lute and an incense jar.
Someday, when you play this lute

or light some incense in this jar, look outside.
If a little breeze is stirring the leaves
and the blades of grass,
think of me. It will mean I've come home.

'Once I promised to entwine
the bamboo with the plum tree,
but this willow is weak. This reed is broken.
And when you hear that I have been swallowed by the night,
pour some water on the ground in memory of the dead.
This hairpin is snapped. This vase is smashed.

'No words can tell how much I love him.
I bow a hundred thousand times before him
to mourn the shortness of our love.
I am poor and treacherous as quicklime.
I am a petal on a swollen stream.
O darling Kim, my darling Kim!
As of today, I have betrayed your love.'

And having spoken, the words choke her.
She faints. Her hands are cold as copper.
Her parents awake at this commotion.
The room is suddenly full of people,
bringing smelling salts and medicine.
When she comes to, her cheeks are still wet.

They ask her what the matter is.
Kiều sobs, but cannot speak a word.
Vân whispers her secret to their parents:
'Here are the bracelets Kim gave her,
and here are their promises of love.'

Her father says, 'I see. Then it is I, your father,
who have forced you to break your vow.
Well, let your sister honour it in your place.

It is my fault that the mustard seed must fly,
that the pin must leave its magnet.
Though the mountains shall crumble,
I will keep my word.'

Kiều bows before him and says,
'If you help me keep my promises,
then I won't care if I become a slave
or if my bones whiten beneath a foreign field.'

How to speak of all her sadness?
From the southern watchtower, a roll of drums
announces the end of the night.

A flower-strewn carriage arrives at the door,
with flutes and lutes, to carry her away.
She does not want to leave;
they do not want to let her leave.
Tears drop on the stone steps.
She is drawn to her family by silken threads.

                              *

That evening, sullen clouds scud across the sky.
Leaves and grasses droop with drops of dew.
The carriage arrives at a tavern. Mã goes for a drink.
He leaves her alone in an empty room.
She is a young girl in the spring.

Kiều is torn between shame and fear.
She remembers how she was wooed by Kim
and the memory makes her suffering worse:
'I used to think I would live for ever,
but now I am the wife of a villain.
I did not let my lover pluck my flower.
I guarded it well from the easterly wind.

I failed him then and make it worse now.
When finally we meet again, there will be nothing left
of my poor body. I am a broken fern
on a swollen stream. How can any woman
live with such a fate?'

There is a knife on the table before her.
She slips it into her sleeve.
'When the worst comes, this knife might help me out.'

The night drags slowly. She dozes,
and thinks about her life
between wake and sleep.

*

What kind of man is Mã, the college graduate?
A drinker, a frequenter of brothels,
a waster who squandered his money on loose living.
And now he earns it back through the only trade he knows –
he runs a brothel with a woman called Mrs Tú
whose charms have declined slightly with the passing years.
Sometimes these nice coincidences work:
he sells snake-oil, she sells slapped-on beauty –
they make a perfect match.
They pool their resources, and open up one of those houses
that sell perfume and powder and related products.
To stock it, he travels the countryside,
looking for nice young girls who have to earn their keep
as servants. But he and Mrs Tú
have a specialized form of service in mind.

Heaven holds our destinies, whether good or bad:
if misery wants you, misery will root you out.
Have pity on this frail woman,
sold at a bargain price to a travelling salesman.

Now she is caught in his bag of tricks:
the pay-off to the family and the pretend wedding.

He is secretly delighted: 'The flag is in my hand –
it's mine to wave! And she is of the finest jade,
the loveliest creature in the land, a natural beauty.
When we set her before our customers
the word will spread for miles around.
Three hundred liạng to be the first in the queue
will almost cover my initial outlay;
everyone that follows gives me clear profit.
Yet she is such a tempting, tasty-looking dish,
I'd love to bite it myself. Except that, seeing she's a virgin,
I'd be throwing away good money.

'A perfect peach, and all I have to do is bend the branch,
bring it to my lips and teeth, and taste the juice.
And those thick peasants, my customers,
how many of them can judge a flower?
A drop or two of chicken blood, a dash of pomegranate juice,
and she will be good as new.
She'll fool some swarthy farmer in the half-light:
three hundred liạng to be first in the queue,
and not a penny less.
And if my old lady suspects something,
I'll just have to face the music.
Here's another point. We're still so far from home,
that if I don't make a move,
the girl will start to wonder
what exactly is going on.'

And that is how a pure camellia
is forced to let the bee explore her every petal,
inside and out. His dreadful storm breaks
over her flawless jade, he drowns her tender perfume.
This long spring night becomes a single nightmare.

She wakes alone in the torchlight, and her tears begin again.
She hates the stranger and she hates her own skin.
She thinks, 'This is horrible. My body was once
purer than spun gold, and as rare, but now
that purity is gone, along with my honour.
So that's the end. There's nothing left to hope for.
A dishonoured life is worth nothing at all.'

And so she takes the knife out of her gown.
She thinks: 'If I were alone,
I could end it here. But I must think of my family.
An inquest into my suicide
might require them to repay the wedding fee.
Perhaps this life will become bearable in time.
We die only once.'

She balances these questions
until the cocks crow at the break of dawn.
The watchtower horn sounds across the morning mist.
Outside, Mã is ordering that the horses be saddled.

The melancholy sounds of leaving your homeland:
hooves upon the hard road,
wheels rattling along the ruts.

*

Ten miles outside town is the spot
her father has booked for a farewell party.
While the guests are celebrating
Kiều goes to meet her mother in an inner room.
Their tears are hot, but their eyes speak.

Kiều says: 'Mother, I am just a girl
and I can never repay what you have done for me.
But in this unjust world,

clear water turns dirty
while the muck calls itself clean.
Though I live a hundred years
I will carry you all in my heart.
But from what I have seen, these last few days,
I think I have fallen into the hands of a liar and a cheat.
When we arrived at the inn, he abandoned me.
He was awkward and rough coming into my room,
and afterwards, he couldn't wait to get away.
You can't have a decent conversation with him.
His men despise him. He commands no respect.
He doesn't talk or act like a civilized person.
Watch him for yourself: he talks like a salesman.
There's nothing more to say.
Your daughter must live in an uncouth country
and sleep in a strange man's room.'

Mrs Vương lets out a wail that would reach heaven,
demanding vengeance.

The guests have not even finished their drinks
when Mã is outside, harnessing the horses.
Kiều's father has a heavy heart about his daughter's fate.
The old man stands beside Mã's saddle and says:
'Because our family has met with certain difficulties,
my daughter has agreed to be your concubine or slave;
and now, beyond the sea, at the sky's edge,
she'll pass each lonely day among strangers.
But I ask you to be her mighty oak.
Let your branches protect her from frost and snow.'

The bridegroom says, 'My feet are tied to hers
by the sacred thread of matrimony.
The sun is my witness. If I'm telling a lie,
let all the demons prick me with their swords.'

And the coach roars away, a miniature storm
churning up clouds of red dust.
Kiều's parents dry their eyes and watch it speed away.

For many days afterwards, they often look
along the road that her carriage took.

ba

bà: grandmother
bá: uncle; or to embrace
bả: poison; or bait
bã: rubbish
bạ: at random
ba: dad; or three

3

She travels impossibly far, across bridges
powdered with hoar frost, past forests
glowering with broody clouds, through fields
of rumour-monger reeds, whispering and wild,
raked by the knife of a north wind
that ruffles their reed-heads to a skittering sea.

And still the road reels out before her.

She crosses unnamed bridges, climbs unguessed-of hills,
through autumnal forests where red and amber
stain the blue-green leaves. The cries of sad birds
remind her of the family she has left behind.
By night, the witnessing moon looks down
and she remembers her now-broken vows.
It waxes and it wanes till they reach Linzi.

The beaded carriage creaks to a halt before a gate.
A woman waddles out to greet them.
Her face is skimmed with rice-powder paste;
Kiều wonders what kind of diet
enables a person to get so fat.
She greets Kiều with a bustling 'Hello, how are you?'
and helps her out of the carriage. Kiều follows
where the woman leads, and steps inside the house.

The room is full of people. Along one wall,
girls sit with eyebrows plucked and pencilled;
along the other, four or five smirking men.
In the centre is an altar lined with smoking incense
and, above it, the image of that grinning hairy god
who is worshipped in such green pavilions:[23]
the faithful bring him flowers. They burn candles day and night.

If an unlucky girl runs out of customers,
she should come to this god, strip off all her clothes,
kneel, light incense, say a prayer,
then gather up the faded blooms. If she does
all this, many customers will follow. Those bees will buzz.

Kiều knows nothing of such places. She kneels
where she is told to kneel, while her hostess prays:

'May luck and looks and money rain on this house!
May we dance all day and smooch all night!
May every man be smitten with our new girl,
may orioles and swifts now flock to find us –
may poems and love letters pour through our door!
May they queue at the front door, may they queue at the back!'

This all sounds strange to Kiều's bewildered ears.
She wonders now what kind of place this is.
After her prayers, the old one settles on the couch.
She says, 'Come and kneel before me now. I'm your Auntie Tú.
In the next room, you'll kowtow before your uncle Mã.'

'Bad luck banished me from my home,' says Kiều.
'To pay my father's debts, I agreed to play this role,
but it seems you want this swift to be an oriole.
I'm too young to understand how this business works.
But Mã paid us bridal gifts; there was a wedding;
I thought I was a concubine. I've shared my husband's bed.
Please explain more clearly if I've a different role instead.'

When Mrs Tú hears these words, three demons leap out of her.

'A concubine!' she says. 'A concubine then, is it?
I see now what my aul fella's done. I send him out shopping
to bring me a girl – a pretty girl, I told him, a nice little girl –
and he sends me a creature that thinks she's his wife,

or his half-wife, or whatever they're calling it these days.
I'll teach that gobshite the meaning of the word concubine.
That half-witted chancer, that prick-for-brains,
him and his shagging itch, he had to scratch it,
he couldn't leave it well alone, he had to put his bloody mitts
all over my brand new tablecloth. I might as well
have thrown my money out the window
as trust it to that gormless ape. And as for you,
Miss Flibbertigibbet, I've paid for you,
you're in my house, and you'll do what you're damn well told.
What were you thinking, to let him have his way?
An old lech like him? Why didn't you slap his face?
You're a bold young girl with a one-track mind,
and now you'll feel the lick of my switch.'
She grabs a whip and prepares to crack it.

Kiều says, 'O endless skies! O vast earth!
I threw my life away when I left home:
now I have nothing left to live for.'

She slips the hidden knife out of her sleeve.
Horribly, she finds the courage to stab herself.
The madam hides her face in her hands.

But are such beauty and talent to come to an end,
to be severed by the blade of a knife?
There is a commotion. People pour into the room.
Kiều is unconscious, covered with blood.
Mrs Tú stands and shakes, scared half to death.
Kiều is carried out to a western room.
Someone cradles her head. They call a doctor.

She is not quite dead. Near comatose,
she senses a girl come to her side
who whispers: 'Your time has not yet come.
You cannot escape your duties to the world of sadness.

Your cheeks are still as fresh as peaches.
You want to leave this life, but heaven will not let you.
So live. Follow your destiny, frail reed.
I'll meet you some day, by the Qiantang river.'[24]

They give her balms and medicines all day
and Kiều slowly regains consciousness.
Mrs Tú is waiting by her mosquito net
to reassure her with these soothing words:
'Child, we have only one life to live,
and you are a young girl with your spring days
still ahead of you. I made a bad mistake.
It was wrong of me to try to force you
into the art of making clouds and rain,
since you are faithful as stone and gold.
But since some unlucky path has led you to our door,
we'll give you your own room, one you can lock,
where you can wait for a nice man to marry you.
I'll find you a good one, don't worry.
But don't bring harm to me, who meant no harm to you.
If you kill yourself, that would make me very sad.'

Kiều listens to these wheedling words
and finds a kind of logic to them.
She remembers the message she heard in her dream:
heaven often takes a hand in human affairs.
If she doesn't settle her debts in this life,
she'll have to settle them in the next.

She weighs up her dilemma.
She tells Mrs Tú, 'Nobody wants life
to turn out like this. If you'll keep your promise,
then I'll do as you ask and I'll count myself lucky.
But will what you do tomorrow match what you say today?
I've known too many bees and butterflies.
I'd rather die clean than live in a ditch.'

The madam answers: 'Child, don't worry.
I wouldn't have the heart to trick you.
The sun is my witness. If I'm telling a lie,
let that be my judge and my punishment.'

This solemn vow sets Kiều's mind at rest,
and slowly she drifts into sleep.

                         *

They give her a private room in the Turquoise Retreat.
Her companions are the moon, some distant hills,
a certain line of trees. From all four windows,
she looks towards the horizon across golden dunes,
along the pink dust of the sand trails.
She feels shame at the sight of the dawn clouds,
shame at the glow of the midnight lamp:
everything reminds her of that recent night
when her lover was beside her in the moonlight
as they shared wine from a single jade cup.
Now he travels under distant skies,
hoping the rain will drip with news of her.
Stranded alone in this strange land,
how can she empty her heart of love?
She thinks of her parents, waiting by their door.
Who will fan them when they get hot
or warm their blankets when they feel the cold?
The young catalpa tree in the family yard
must be wide enough now to embrace.

Sadness in the harbour in the afternoon
when a tall ship slips far away.
Sadness in the rivers that run to the sea,
in the flowers that drift in the current.
Sadness in the shimmer of wilting grass
where land meets sky and everything turns blue.

Sadness in the wind that whips about the cove,
in the waves that crash against the headland.
Alone among alien rivers and foreign hills,
she writes homesick songs of exile.

One evening, drawing her curtain, she hears
a stranger's voice from the room next door
reciting some of her own poems.

Curious, she goes into the next room.
She finds a well-dressed bookish young man
holding forth about poetry.
Someone tells her his name is Sở Khanh.
They say he fell in love with Kiều's silhouette
when he saw it framed against the curtain.

'She is the very queen of beauty,' he is saying.
'And where she walks, the sweetest perfume trails.
She should live on the moon or among the clouds:
so fair a rose does not belong in a dump like this.
My blood boils at heaven for allowing this to happen –
but she can never guess my heart's true feelings.
If only she knew that I am her rescuer.
I can spring her from this trap.
That kind of thing comes easy to a man like me.'

Kiều returns to her room and locks the door,
the echo of those fine words still ringing in her ears.
She thinks of the young man, and thinks of herself.
She no longer feels so alone.

*

Day follows day, waiting and hoping for nothing,
endless as dust that winnows in the wind.

Kiều decides to take a chance. She writes a few lines,
asking the young man to rescue her from these troubled seas.
She explains how she paid her father's debts
and how that transaction brought her to this green pavilion.
At dawn, as the sun breaks through the morning mists,
she asks a maid to carry her note to the stranger.

The sun is setting fire to the western sky
when the young man's answer arrives.
She slits open the fine apricot paper.
She reads two characters – *Wuxi việt* –
which mean 'the growth of Vietnam',
or look at them another way and they say:
'seven o'clock this evening'.

Birds fly home to the twilight woods.
A crescent moon peeps through the camellias.
Branches dance with shadows on the eastern wall.

Kiều opens the curtains:
Sở Khanh is tiptoeing up the steps.
She plucks up the courage to go and greet him.

She says: 'I am a broken piece of waterweed,
fallen among these swifts and orioles.
Will you help me to regain my freedom?
I will repay you with knotted grass and rings of jade.'

He listens, nods and grins. He says,
'You've come to the right man.
You chose the right one to ask for help,
I'll take your sea of troubles and drain it dry.'

'I'll depend on you for everything,' she says.
'Tell me what to do and I will follow your instructions.'

He says, 'My horses run faster than the wind.
My servant is a very strong man.
Let us seize our opportunity and escape.
As the proverb puts it: in difficult times,
there might be thirty-six possible plans,
but the best is always to run like hell.
Also, if by any chance something happens to go wrong
just at the very moment we are trying to escape,
have no fear. I absolutely guarantee
that I will be at your side at that point.'

These words do not fill her with confidence.
Instead, she suspects a trap.
But what does anything matter?
She shuts her eyes and leaps into the abyss,
to learn what the cruel child who made this world
has planned for her this time.

                                        *

Together they creep down the steps.
They leave on horseback, one leading
and the other following.

The autumn night drags its feet.
The wind shudders through the trees.
Yellow leaves sink beneath their hooves.
The moon sets behind distant mountains.
Rain drips along the forest path,
constant as a water clock.
The grass is wet with dew.
With every step, she longs for home.

At dawn, the cocks are crowing when she hears
the shout of an ambush.
Suddenly she is surrounded.

Her heart leaps.
Sở Khanh is nowhere to be seen.
She is alone in the heart of the forest.

Great child that works your magic on this world,
how can you be so cruel?
How can you let this rose be trampled underfoot?

Her captors encircle her, closing in.
She can neither burrow like a mole,
nor fly like a bird.

Auntie Tú appears out of nowhere
to drag her from her horse
and haul her home.

*

No questions, no explanations:
Mrs Tú selects a cane
and flays the flower,
thrashing the lovely willow
in a blind rage.
Beautiful or plain,
it hurts just the same.

Kiều confesses: her head is bloody.
She begs for mercy: her back is torn open.

She says: 'I am a girl. I left the safety of my home
and journeyed over mountains and rivers to flounder here.
You hold the power over my life or death.
I have nothing left to wish for,
my fate is written.
But since you spent the silver to trick me here,
why should you throw it away?

I am an eel that must swim through this silt:
I know that my head will get dirty.
I renounce all hope of staying clean.'

The brothel-keeper seizes on these words.
She sends for pen, paper and a witness:
she plans to make Kiều's despair
legally binding.

One of the working girls, Mã Kiều,
is forced to act as a hostage for Kiều.
If her namesake should escape again,
Mã Kiều will be punished in her stead.
With a mixture of threats and chicanery,
the madam sets the terms of Kiều's parole.

They carry Kiều through to an inner room
and tend to her bleeding wounds.

Mã Kiều says: 'You fell for an old trick.
Round here, we've got the measure of Sở Khanh:
he's known to every brothel for miles around.
He plays the field and plucks the prettiest flowers like you.
That conman and the madam plan their moves together.
It's an old fencing trick: drop your guard,
then jab and stab.
I'd guess she paid him thirty liạng for what he did.
He wouldn't have pulled such a stunt for free.
Now that it's over, he'll deny everything.
Watch what you say. He's a snake:
dangerous when poked.'

Kiều says: 'But he spoke so wonderfully!
How can a man's words be empty as the wind?'

She is still meditating on this question,
when the two-faced betrayer bursts into the room
and gives out the following tirade:
'Tell the truth. I won't have lies told about me.
This little whore is claiming I seduced her,
that I lured the wind and trapped her cloud.
I dare her to say it to my face.'

Kiều answers: 'I have nothing to say.
If you say it never happened, it didn't.'

Sở Khanh curses her in a voice louder than thunder.
He bunches his fists and shapes to hit her.

'Heaven always knows what happens,' says Kiều,
'who lures the swift, who traps the oriole:
who filled a trap with bamboo spikes
and pushed me in it.
God hears who makes vows
and knows who breaks them.
You accuse me of lying.
Look here. I have your note.
It reads, *Wuxi việt*, which means
"seven o'clock this evening".
Whose handwriting is this?
Whose face is in these characters?'

Everyone hears these words, and their truth is plain.
They condemn the traitor and his shameless skulduggery:
he cannot deny the evidence of his own words.
He stammers, gapes and runs away.

*

Alone in her room, she weeps.
She thinks about fate, about life and misfortune:
'The purest snow gets trodden to slush.
The clarity of frost never protects it.
Happiness and misery meet the same end:
no rose exists that blooms for ever.
I must have done something atrocious in a previous life,
for there can be no doubt that I am paying for it now.
My innocence is gone. This vase is broken.
My body must redeem my debt to life.'

The round moon gleams like a mirror.

Mrs Tú comes to see her.
'Love is just a job,' she says. 'It's hard work,
but it brings its pleasures too.
Let me teach you its artistry.'

'My life is caught in a storm,' says Kiều.
'Let the wind whip. Let the rain lash.'

The madam says: 'Rule one: men are all the same.
Give them pleasure and they're sure to come back.
But there's more ways to give pleasure than you ever
        dreamed of.
Play hide-and-seek at night, and cupboard love by day.
There are exactly seven steps to seduce a man.
First you must weep. Then, have your name tattooed on
        his skin.
Talk next about marriage and then about suicide.
Make plans to run away with him.
Cut off a lock of your hair and mingle it with his.
Finally, exchange vows of eternal love.
There are also eight ways to please a man in bed,
depending on whether he is skinny or muscular,
hot-blooded or lackadaisical, experienced or a virgin,

romantic-minded or hard-nosed about money.
I'll explain all those techniques in good time.
You have to love men until they're exhausted,
until their heads spin, until the hardest heart is forced to melt.
I will teach you how to win them with a sidelong glance;
how to use your lips and tongue to your advantage;
how to sing about the moon; and I will teach you
some intimate games to play with flowers.
These are the skills and secrets of our profession.
Learn them, and you'll be made for life.'

Kiều listens to Mrs Tú's words.
Her eyebrows arch. Her face turns white.
Such professional advice is hard to accept
for a girl who grew up in a two-storey house
where women have separate quarters.
Now she must learn a prostitute's trade:
her face will harden and her skin grow dark.
This is as bad as life can get.
Pity this girl, alone in a filthy world,
trapped in the clutches of strangers.

They take down her curtains in the green pavilion.
The higher the price of jade, the more valued it is:
bees and butterflies swarm about the new rose.
An orgy starts one night, and it lasts for a month:
each night there is laughter until dawn.
Branches welcome birds until the leaves sway.
Song Yu arrives as the sun comes up
and Sima Xiangru takes over at nightfall.[25]

But late at night, when she sobers up,
Kiều cries herself to sleep.
Once she was coddled in silk and brocade;
now the torn rose lies trampled by the roadside.
Her smooth face is weathered by wind and rain;

butterflies and bees swarm over her body.
She lets them make clouds over Chu,
she lets them make rain over Qin.
She never feels the sweetness of spring.

Sometimes she collects flowers in the dawn mist,
or watches snow half-cover the windows
as moonlight fills the yard with milk.
Anything cheerful makes her sadder.
When a person is in despair
no loveliness can lift their spirits.

Sometimes she paints, or writes a verse,
or plays her lute in the moonlight,
or plays chess beneath the trailing flowers.
This helps her pass a moment or two,
but none of these pleasures is real.
Where can she find a true friend
who might understand her heart?

She cares neither for the poetry of the wind
through the rustling bamboo
nor for the thin rain on the plum trees.

A hundred worries swirl about her.
When she thinks of the past or the present,
her heart is shredded like torn silk,
her memories are blisters.

She misses her parents.
She owes them the nine thanks
for the nine labours:
for giving birth to her, breastfeeding her,
lovingly caressing her,
weaning her onto solids,
providing her with food,

teaching her, caring about her,
supervising her, and protecting her.
Their lives are fading
like the shadows of mulberry trees at dusk.

At the other end of the long road,
beyond the deepest rivers and the furthest hills,
how can they know what has happened to their daughter?
And what of her brother and sister –
who will guide those younger ones?

She remembers her vow
to love Kim for ever in this life,
or failing that, the next life,
or failing that, the one after that.
In one of those three existences,
she is obliged to love him.

Does Kim know what has happened to her?
When he comes home, will he ask for the willow
from Chương Terrace? They will tell him how the willow
has been ripped from the tree
and that men now pass it from hand to hand.
She hopes that his love can be restored,
as blossoms are grafted back onto a branch.

The ribbon of her thoughts is hopelessly entangled.
At night, from the moment she closes her eyes,
she returns to her homeland,
but she wakens into exile.

Lonely, she looks through her curtained window,
and watches each dusk chase its day.
As the moon-hare leaps, as the sun-crow whirls,
she thinks of the Company of Sadness.

Each member is granted the beauty of a rose
and pays for it in misery.
They live their lives in a fierce sandstorm.
They cannot reach their destiny
until they drink from the cup of grief.

bốn

bon: to hurry
bôn: bolshy (shortened form of Bolshevik)
bợn: flaw
bỗn: washbasin or flower-bed
bòn: to save every scrap, even the tiniest amount
bón: dung
bọn: a gang
bốn: four

4

One day, a handsome merchant – young Mr Thúc –
visits their green pavilion.
Hailing from Wuxi,[26] in the province of Jiangsu,
he has come to Linzi to assist his father –
Mr Thúc senior – in opening a trading post.

He has heard many stories about Kiều's beauty.
He writes to her on pink paper,
inviting himself to her perfumed bedroom.

And now, behind the tasselled drapes, he views her.
He savours every petal of her flower.
The camellia shivers on its stem,
growing more lovely with each spring shower.

Flower and moon, moon and flower:
a passionate embrace on a spring night.
Nothing can sever
the knot that binds two lovers together.

Kiều and Thúc feed each other peaches by day
and plums by night.
Beginning as wind and moonlight,
their love deepens to stone and gold.

Thúc senior has to go back to Jiangsu,
leaving his son in charge of the trading post.
Young Thúc cannot believe his luck.
He loses all sense of time,
spending each day with his lover.

In the cool breeze of a balcony
or in a moonlit garden,
they sip the finest wines
and invent poetry.

They sit side by side
and breathe the smells of dawn,
or the gentle aromas
of green tea at noon.

They play a game of Go
or make duets on their lutes.
They can think of nothing else
except being in love.

Her beauty is a tidal wave
that topples city walls.
Young Thúc would spend two fortunes
on a single smile.

And Mrs Tú begins to smooth Kiều's hair
and to bring her the finest soap.
The madam has an excellent nose
for the delicate smell of money.

And the cuckoos' two-note song
welcomes the summer moon,
while against a corner wall,
pomegranates catch fire.

And one quiet evening
in her private room
he watches her
as she lets the towel fall

to take a perfumed bath
in a soft pool of orchids,
and her body
is jade and ivory,

and while she is naked
she is the finest work
that heaven has created.
And he gazes,

O, he gazes,
and he swoons with delight,
and he sings with love
till he makes a Đường-style poem.

'I like to hear your poems,' she says.
'Each word is hard, like a pearl
or a piece of polished jade.
Each line is a perfect tapestry.

'I wish I could match you,
but my heart is too full
of my homeland.
I have no poems tonight.'

'That's a strange thing to say,' says Thúc.
'I thought here was your home.
And I thought you belonged
to the redoubtable Mrs Tú.'

Her eyes lose their sparkle.
She thinks of her harsh destiny:
'I am a blossom that has fallen from its tree,
and you are a butterfly.

'I'm sure a prince of spring like you
has a princess at home somewhere.
And all these pretty words we say
are nothing but conversation.'

'Since the moment I first saw you,' he says,
'I have felt only love for you:
the kind of love that a man will swear
so that mountains and rivers can hear.

'But you're right. If I want to love you
for a hundred years, then you and I
must follow my stream
back to its source.'

'That's kind of you,' she says.
'But I see some problems.
You looked for me in a green pavilion,
which means you love me for my looks alone.

'Some day these looks will coarsen,
and so will your words.
Also, we both know there's a Chang'e[27]
who lives on your moon,

'and you have tied a knot with her
which I will never sever.
I'm a drifting cloud, a broken fern.
I cannot unmake another woman's love.

'But if that knot unravels of its own accord,
who will be to blame?
If you guide your house with a firm hand,
you might think you will protect me,

'but sometimes the power inside the house
is greater than the husband knows:
I would become a tethered goat
before a lioness's jaws.

'In your house, I would stoop and creep:
that would burn me worse than fire.
The empress Wu
pickled the concubines in vinegar.

'Worse than your wife – think of your father,
the sheltering cedar.
He will not want a willow from the roadside,
nor a rose that you plucked from the wall.

'If he finds you with a girl from a green pavilion,
he will send her back to that same pavilion.
And I will return to this mire again
and you will have lost your good name.

'Only if you are sure that you
can arrange these details perfectly
will I agree to travel to your home
and to do as you ask.'

He says, 'But you speak of these imaginings
as if we are strangers.
Those fearful threats are further
than the furthest fields of Laos.

'With me at your side,
you can smile at those far dangers.
My promises are stone and gold,
stronger than wind or wave.'

And the two exchange loving secrets
for the mountains and rivers to hear.
But this night is too short for love songs:
its moon-hare will soon disappear.

*

They walk out of that green pavilion,
explaining they wish to take a midnight stroll
through the bamboo forest.

Thúc takes Kiều to a safe house
and begins to map out his strategy
to rescue her from the green pavilion.

He would prefer to do things peacefully
but he is prepared for war.
He sends a go-between to Mrs Tú,
to explain how the land now lies.

The madam sees she is beaten:
she negotiates a price.
Thúc pays the required ransom
and informs the local bailiffs.

And so Kiều steps out of the web of men and laws
that had enmeshed her at Linzi.

And the bamboo and the plum tree are entwined
till their love grows deeper than the ocean.
The longer their incense burns,
the fiercer are its flames.
Her loveliness is polished jade.
Her scent is sweeter than jasmine.

*

They live for half a year as man and wife
as the leaves turn yellow, as the twigs turn black,
as the hedges are speckled with frost.

Until that cedar tree arrives on horseback.

Thúc's father is furious. He roars like thunder.
He vows to cleave them asunder.
His verdict is plain:
Send her back to that green pavilion
that she scuttled out from under.

The son stands up to his father. He says:
'I have sinned immeasurably. Strike me
with thunderbolts or machetes and I will accept
these punishments as just. But I have dipped
my hand in indigo, the deeply blue-black dye
that cannot be washed off. What's done is done.
Even if I had played this lute for just a single day,
I would never break its strings.
I do not care what the future brings:
you will have to kill me before I abandon my love.'

Such stubbornness enrages the old man further:
he heads directly to the bailiffs.
A stormy sea now sweeps across the lovers' land:
a scarlet warrant is signed for their arrest.
They walk behind the bailiffs to the court,
where they are forced to kowtow.
They raise their heads to see the judge:
his face is black as iron.
He is known to be a harsh man.

'I see you've been a wild young buck,' says the judge.
'Dragged into court by your own father.
But you, young lady, are a patent fraud,
a withered bloom, all stale perfume and face paint.

Your powder and rouge might swindle dark-skinned farmers,
but it has no such effect on me.
I have studied the complaint.
The case hinges on the character of a girl
whose use of artifice and make-up
provides compelling evidence of her guilt.
I therefore offer you the following choice:
either accept the full punishment
that the law recommends in cases such as yours,
or – more simply and less painfully – return
to that green pavilion whence you came.'

Kiều answers: 'My mind is already made up.
The fly never returns to the spider's web.
Through the thickest slime, through awful suffering,
the sufferer remains a human being.
Let your sentence be carried out.'

The judge instructs that she be fitted
with the three wooden implements of restraint:
shackles, handcuffs and cangue.
She does not shout her innocence,
though tears dampen her cheeks
and her features are twisted with pain.
In the dirt of the courtroom floor,
her face is mired with dust,
her body is thin as an apricot branch.

Think of how this looks to Thúc,
as he watches from a distance,
his entrails skewered by guilt.

He says, 'Her suffering is all my fault.
She foresaw that such a torment
would result from my loving proposal.
I could not grasp what she meant:
now I am forced to watch her cruel fate.'

The judge listens to this lament
and asks the young man to explain his story.
The lover weeps, but through his sobs,
repeats what Kiều had once predicted,
and how he had sworn to protect her,
and how his failure to keep that promise
had brought a life of moonlight and flowers
to the dirt of a courtroom floor.

The judge reflects upon these words
and considers their meaning.
'Moonlight waxes and wanes,' he says.
'Flowers bloom and fade:
but a woman of moonlight and flowers
can still tell right from wrong.'

'She may be only a woman,' adds Thúc,
'but she writes the finest poetry.'

The judge laughs and says, 'Poetry? My God!
You've found a perfect gem.
Then show us, girl – write us a poem
on the subject of your punishment:
tell us how it feels to be clapped in a cangue.'

They unshackle her and give her paper and brush.
She works swiftly and places the page on the judge's desk.

The judge reads them. He is amazed. He says:
'These lines are more heart-rending
than the finest works of the Thịnh Đường poets.
There is not gold enough on earth
to buy a woman of such genius.
This fine young man has made the perfect match.
The families of Châu and Trần were justly famous
for the excellence of their intermarriages,
but they never could have hoped for such a height.

Let us call a halt to these fractious proceedings.
Our purpose should be love, not litigation.
When people bring their troubles to a court of law
they find the home of justice built on mercy.
You brought this case because you feared to lose a son,
but you have found an incomparable daughter.'

His closing verdict is that the two should wed.
The court rickshaw is strewn with flowers
and is carried on the wind, to chase the stars.
A band of pipes and flutes and pounding drums
escorts the bride and groom to their wedding place.
Thúc senior admires his new daughter's poetry
and will not hear another word against her.

And their home is scented with lilies and orchids.
Misery makes way for love.

                                    *

The days slip by with wine and chess.
Peaches ripen and fall; the lotus throws new shoots.
One quiet evening in a curtained room,
Kiều tells her husband what is troubling her.

'Since you first rescued this frail fledgling,
geese have followed swallows across the sky.
One year has passed, without a word from your home.
You've grown closer to this clinging vine,
and forgotten the woman you married
when you were living off wine dregs and rice husks.
Think of how this must look to others:
every gossip talks for hours about our friendship.
I hear that your first wife is most correct
and does everything by the book.
I fear that kind of straightness. It is hard to guess

what lies at the bottom of her ocean.
We have lived together for a full year.
It is obvious that she must know about us,
and holds her opinion, and yet
you have received not a single message from her:
her silence is what shouts the loudest.
You must go home immediately.
That will please her.
And we'll learn what she is thinking.
You might think that you are playing
a harmless game of hide-and-seek,
but remember the one who hides in that game
is also the one who gets found out.'

Thúc reflects on these unhurried words
that mark the crux of their predicament.
He visits the house of the cedar tree.
His father agrees that he should make the trip.

And so they leave their spring villa
for the mountain post of Gaoting,
where they plan to drink a parting cup
and bid each other goodbye for perhaps a year.
The banks of the thin blue ribbon of the Qin
are strewn with willow branches
from the Yang Pass:[28]
beyond that western pass live only strangers.
The lovers sigh; they hold hands.
They cannot touch the final glass,
nor bring themselves to utter
that fatal word: Farewell.

'Mountains and rivers may come between us,'
says Kiều, 'but your home must be warmed within
if we are to live quietly without.
Pay attention or you will miss the red flags waving:

look closely and you can thread a needle's eye.
The grass stirs wherever a man walks.
Nobody catches birds with his eyes closed.
The thread that binds us now is weak:
go home, explain our position to your wife.
See what she thinks. If she creates a storm,
tell her I know my place and will honour hers.
It is better to be honest about where we stand
than to lie and hide and sow problems for the future.
Lover, if you love me, hear these words.
A year is a long time, but that year will pass.
So let us drain this parting glass,
in honour of the happier cup we'll share
twelve months from now.'

Thúc mounts his horse and she lets go of his gown.
The maple woods take on the colours of autumn,
the shades of long roads and mountain passes.
As he rides away, the dust swirls up and settles
among the green mulberry groves.
Kiều turns away to face her night alone:
alone he rides through dark and silence.

What happened to the lovers' moon?
It washes the pillow where she rests her head.
It gleams upon his distant path.

*

Who knows what thoughts trouble that horseman?
Let us turn to the woman who rules his home.
Her name is Hoạn. Her family is powerful:
her father heads the civil government.
A happy wind once blew Thúc into her arms
and then they tied the sacred marriage knot.
Her own perfection makes it easy
for her to see the faults in others.

So there's a newly bloomed rose in his garden:
she has heard it from everyone's lips except his.
And the anger smoulders in her charcoal heart
against the husband who left her for moonlight and flowers.

'If only he had confessed it, if he had told me the truth,
I would have managed to be gracious.
I could have made room for that slattern.
Why would I give up my excellent reputation
to take on the role of the jealous wife?
But he chose to play such a childish trick.
He thinks I don't know what he gets up to
when he's far away. I know that game.
You hide, I count to a hundred.
And you might be surprised at what I'll find.
The ant is crawling around the rim of the cup.
When I am done with them, they won't be able
to stand the sight of each other. I'll crush her.
I'll rub his face in it. I'll make him regret
that he was so quick to sell his old boat
before he'd bought the timber for a new one.'

She lets these thoughts fester in her heart,
while rumours drift serenely past her ears.
Two neighbours bring the story
of what the dogs in the street are saying.
They hope for a reward. She screams at them:
'I loathe this kind of tittle-tattle.
My husband would not behave like that.
These lies are the frothing of foul mouths.'

Her servant boxes the ears of one
and hits the other so hard he knocks out her tooth.
After that incident, silence descends on the house:
nobody dares speak another word.

Hoạn spends all her days in a rose-painted room,
chatting and laughing as if nothing is wrong,
though her blood blisters and boils.

And then he comes home, just like that.
He arrives at the door of her rose-painted room.
They are happy to see each other:
they inquire about each other's health
and talk about the weather.

It begins again: those old feelings of love.
They break open the wine, and smile and chat,
but nobody can read what lies behind their eyes.

His plan is to find out what his wife knows and thinks,
and then tactfully to explain his version of the truth.
But every time he tries to find the words,
she simply laughs and changes the subject.
She never gives the slightest sign
that she knows about his affair.

He can't believe his luck. He thinks:
'I'll keep my thumb on the top of the bottle:
why confess, when she's not even asking questions?'
And therefore he havers and dithers about,
fearful that the whole forest might shake
if he starts to tug at a vine.

Sometimes, in all the banter and the badinage,
she drops a little hint. A dig. She says:
'You and I know jade from stone, and gold from brass.
We trust each other absolutely.
Of course I've heard stories: chattering tongues
that say you play with butterflies and bees.
I never listen to such nonsense.

If I did, I might have become a laughing stock.'
She makes it sound like a joke, an off-hand remark,
and he replies in kind, keeping it light and easy.

And they flirt and chuckle in the moonlight.
And a hundred shadows mingle
beside the midnight lantern.

                              *

He starts getting used to home cooking:
milkfish and watercress. The plane trees
drop golden leaves down the well.
He remembers his life beyond the mountain pass
where he had loved Kiêu through all four seasons.
Before he can utter a word, his wife guesses
what is on his mind. She says, casually:
'It has been a year since you saw those white clouds.
You should head back to Linzi for a while,
to take care of your old father.'

These words untie the knot that binds his heart.
He leaps on his horse and rides swiftly
across rivers and mountains,
towards that distant country.

Along the road, floodwater mirrors the sky.
Blue mists swirl around drystone walls.
Far mountains turn golden with the sun.

                              *

No sooner has he cracked the whip and spurred the horse
than his wife takes the coach to see her mother.
She explains to that tiger lily the whole story:
how he had cheated, then lied about the cheat,

and how she had borne that insult in silence.
'Two things hurt worse the more you scratch,'
she says. 'A mangy itch, and jealousy.
To shout and stamp might have made him feel bad,
but it would have made me look worse.
So I said nothing. I pretended not to see.
And in silence I mapped out my strategy.
To reach Linzi by road takes one month,
but less if you cut across the sea.
I'll send a boat. I have one or two useful servants.
I'll have them bring her back in chains.
Let her suffer, for a change. Let her go half-mad.
Let her be reduced to a wretchedness so intense
she can taste it in her mouth, like blood.
I want to lance my own hatred:
may its pus burst all over them.
Let them become the laughing stock
of every gossip in the country.'

'What an excellent plan!' says her mother.
'Have the girl sent to me.'

With this parental collaboration, Hoạn feels free
to rig a junk with the strongest rope
and the swiftest sails. She gives her henchmen –
the one called Dog, the one called Sparrowhawk –
precise instructions as to what they must do.

And the boat flies like a leaf in the wind
over the flat sea, towards Linzi.

                          *

Kiều sits and watches the rain.
Sadness trickles down her heart
like raindrops on the glass.

'The shadows are fading on my parents.
They are mulberry trees at twilight.
Have they warm clothes? Have they enough to eat?

'Once I cut my hair for Kim,
now it reaches past my shoulders.
What happened to our loving vows
that the rivers and mountains could hear?
I live my life as a clinging vine
in a half-marriage you could hardly call
the perfect square or circle.
My days bring misery. My nights bring sadness.
I wish I could live like Chang'e
in her cold palace on the moon.'

Autumn night: a soft breeze plays at her window.
High in the sky, a crescent moon with three stars
resembles the character for Thúc's name.

She steps into the courtyard,
where there is a makeshift altar.
She burns a few sticks of incense.
She kneels to say her prayers.

The moment she starts to meditate,
a gang of thugs break out of their hiding places
from under the hanging flowers.
They shriek and howl and whoop
till the night air shimmers with a deafening shrillness
that would have terrified the devil himself,
and the blackness glimmers with scimitars.

Kiều is astounded. They fall upon her
and press her face into a concoction
brewed from soporific herbs.
She falls unconscious in an instant.

They sling her over the back of a horse
and set fire to Thúc's library and to her own inner room.
By a villainous coincidence,
they had found a drowned woman floating in the river,
and they drag this corpse into the burning building.

Kiều's servants have scattered.
They hide in the bushes,
scared out of their wits.
Old man Thúc awakes – he lives in the neighbourhood.
Recognizing the source of the flames, he leaps into action.
He brings men and organizes a water chain
to quench the fire and to look for Kiều.
The wind whips up and the flames grow higher.
All the servants are accounted for.
Frantic, with wild eyes and unkempt hair,
they search every shrub. They peer down the well.
She is nowhere to be found.
As the flames die, they battle through the smoke
towards her inner room.
There they find how we all must end:
a shroud of ashes, a bony frame charred black.
Honest minds imagine no evil:
they name the nameless body Kiều.

Old man Thúc falls to his knees and weeps.
He mourns the lovely girl his absent son has lost.
He gathers up the bones and ashes and brings her home.
He covers her with a sheet
and places her in a coffin
and buries her in the decent earth.

*

The funeral is over. Kiều is dead and buried
when Thúc arrives on horseback
from the long trek over land.
He steps into the very room
where she once made and murmured poetry.
He finds nothing but a floor of cinders
and four blackened, rain-beaten walls.

He hurries to his father's house.
There, in the middle room, stands an altar
whose tablet bears the name of the deceased:
Vương Thúy Kiều.

He learns the awful story.
Love lacerates his heart.
Anguish burns his belly.
He falls to the ground and weeps.

'How could death have come for such a woman?
I thought the plum tree and the bamboo
would never become untwined.
I never dreamed that we'd already said
farewell for ever.'

Love sharpens his thoughts,
and the very sharpness causes him more pain.
Nothing can extinguish
the blazing furnace of his grief.

He hears that a wise man lives nearby
who can summon devils from their jet-black world.
He can visit the Three Islands and the Yellow Springs
to find where the ancestors are wandering.
Thúc sends gifts to welcome this teacher,
and asks him to make inquiries about her.

The wise man kneels before an outdoor altar.
He lights a few sticks of incense,
and then his soul leaves his body.
He reappears a few minutes later,
before the incense has quite burned itself out.

'I did not meet the girl herself,' he says,
'but the ghosts told me about her fate.'
His report is clear and precise.
'She is not dead. She is obliged to live
as one of the Company of Sadness,
and still must endure further torments.
You will meet her again one year from today,
but there will be a strangeness when you meet:
each of you will long to look upon the other,
but neither will dare.'

This prophecy sounds bizarre to Thúc:
he should not have wasted his time with such a charlatan.
The shaman's words make no sense:
how can Kiều ever reappear in this world?

Thúc mourns for his lost flower
and weeps because his spring days are now over:
how often do you meet such a girl in real life?

*

The fallen rose has been washed downstream:
true hell is this world of human beings.
Dog and Sparrowhawk, having carried out their plan,
place Kiều on the deck of their hired junk.
They raise the sails and pull tight the halyards
and the ship skims across the waves towards Wuxi.

Dog and Sparrowhawk dock at the harbour.
They head for the palace – Hoạn's parents' house –
to claim their reward. They deliver Kiều,
still unconscious, to the servants' quarters.

Dreaming of plum trees, Kiều awakes
to find a cook stirring a pot of yellow millet.
Whose house is this? How did she get here?
Still half-asleep, she tries to ask these questions,
but her tongue fumbles and her mind is blurred.

From the courtroom at the centre of the house
resounds an imperious voice, calling her name.
The servants nearby urge her to answer.
They pull her to her feet. She stumbles where they lead.

She looks up to find herself in a stately room
whose banner reads: 'The Prime Minister'.
Candles burn in broad daylight on all sides.
A lady sits on a couch inlaid with the seven gems:
gold, silver, lapis lazuli, quartz, coral, pearl and amber.
She instructs Kiều to recount her background and origin.
Kiều answers truthfully. She tells the story of her life.

And then the rainclouds burst. The lady says:
'You shameless vagabond. You adventurer.
You are a runaway slave or a wandering wife.
You are a graveyard cat, a hen from the fields.
The way you stammer and stutter your invented tale
tells us that you are not to be trusted.
How do you dare to speak such precocious lies,
and you an indentured servant to this house?
Do you think we have no discipline here?
Give this liar thirty blows with a bamboo cane.'

With one voice, the servants answer, 'Yes, madam.'
A hundred voices could not have protected Kiều.
The air whoops with the swish of lashing canes
that slash and sting and rip the flesh.
And the sprig of peach, the twig of plum
is savaged and torn by another tempest.

The lady gives Kiều a new name – Slave Flower –
and orders her to start work as a housemaid.
Slave Flower is given the blue clothes of a servant.
Her hair is ragged, her skin is dull as lead.

The palace housekeeper feels sorry for the new slave.
She brings her a cup of tea,
with balm to tend her wounds
and advice on surviving her new role.

'Everything that happens, whether good or bad,
has been written long ago. The willow may be frail,
but it survives the storm.
Someday the weather must improve.
This present suffering might be punishment
for a sin you committed in a previous life,
since every wrong must have its explanation.

'Mud walls have cracks, but all walls listen:
be careful what you say. If you meet an old friend,
turn away. Lightning can strike out of a clear sky.
Ants can never hope for justice.'

Tears like pearls run down Kiều's cheeks,
and she speaks aloud her secret thoughts.
'I have survived the sandstorm,' she says,
'but this swamp is worse than where I was before.
Cruel fate never loosens its grip:
it tightens its hold on rose-cheeked girls.

If I must redress some unknown crimes,
then let me endure whatever is fit.
Flowers will fade. Jade will splinter.'

Kiều has been working in the palace for a few days
when Hoạn arrives to visit her parents.
Mother and daughter discuss various matters
in private. The mother sends for Slave Flower.

'My daughter requires a slave to tend her every need.
You must now leave me, to become her maidservant.'

Kiều follows her new mistress, uncertain
whether this path will lead to heaven or to hell.
Day and night, she hands the young woman combs and towels.
She comes whenever she is called.
She becomes the perfect slave.

One quiet evening, Hoạn asks Slave Flower
if she can play any bamboo instruments
with their silky strings.
Kiều tunes a lute and begins to strum.

Liquid music pours out of that moon-bowl:
gentle consolation for a maimed soul.
Hoạn's heart is lulled by the lilting sound
and, just for a moment, her hard face softens.

Kiều continues serving in the stranger's house,
though her only friend is her own shadow.
She thinks of her husband in Linzi.
The water fern has lost that friendly river:
they may not meet again in this life.
Heaven is a great mass of white clouds.
She searches it, but never finds her home.

*

As the months roll by, with troubles of his own,
Thúc does not suspect what has happened far away.
Linzi is loveless and empty for him now:
he sleeps alone in a silent bedroom.
He sees her eyebrow in the arc of the moon;
the night jasmine recalls her perfume.

The lotus dies: chrysanthemums throw shoots.
Grief weakens over time: winter turns to spring.
He tells himself that the calendar is a circle
and that cruel fate cannot be changed.
This softens his pain.

He grows nostalgic for his first wife
and makes the long journey home.

She greets him at the gate, delighted:
she has been longing to see him.
They inquire about each other's health,
and the changeable weather.

Once indoors, Hoạn opens the curtains
to fill the room with daylight.
She summons Slave Flower
to greet her new master.

Kiều falters as she enters the room.
Perhaps she is dazzled by the sunlight,
but there, seated at the far end,
seems to be her own husband, Thúc.

Then she thinks: 'Now I understand
how she has caught me in her trap.
But how could such an evil plan
have been concocted by a woman?

'Once we were husband and wife;
now we are master and slave.
And she has worked that transformation
with treacherous perfection.

'She smiled at me. She pretended
to be my friend. But all the while
she was preparing to slit my throat
without using a knife.

'And there is nothing I can do
while she sits so high –
no more than the trampled dirt
can challenge the sky.'

Staring at Thúc, she feels as if a silkworm
has burrowed into the cocoon of her heart
to unravel it thread by thread.
But she must obey her mistress.
She bows, and kneels, and kowtows.
Thúc is thunderstruck.

'Kiều, my own Kiều, is alive,
and kneels here before me.
But we are snared in a trap
and I know who designed it.'

He dare not speak,
nor even show that he knows her.
Yet hiding these feelings
brings tears to his eyes.

'My dear, you seem upset.
Whatever is the matter?
I thought you would be feeling
happy to be home.'

'I was remembering my mother,' he says.
'Sometimes I climb the bare hills
and think of her, until my heart hurts
to the ends of the skies.'

'How sweet!' she says.
'What a dutiful son!
Let's have a glass of wine
to celebrate your homecoming.'

The husband and wife drink
to his return, and to the end of autumn.
Slave Flower is required
to replenish each glass.

Her mistress finds fault with her,
makes her kneel to offer each drink.
Thúc appears demented,
he scarcely knows where to look.

As the hours pass, he talks too much,
and forces himself to laugh.
He claims to be tired, and drunk.
He asks to retire.

'Slave!' says his wife. 'Persuade my husband
to drain his cup, or I will have you thrashed.'
Though the taste is sour as soapberry,
he downs it and tries to look glad.

His wife laughs, acting tipsy.
She commands another drink.
She suggests the perfect entertainment
to liven up the evening.

'Slave Flower is only a servant,' she says,
'but she plays the lute quite skilfully.'
She turns to Kiều, who burns with shame.
'Slave, play something pretty for your master.'

Kiều bows and takes up the lute
and kneels before the thin gauze screen.
As she tunes the four strings,
sad notes loom into the dark like sobs.

How differently the listeners hear them!
One glows with the warmth of victory:
the other is wracked with grief and guilt.
He turns his head to hide his tears.

The mistress shouts again at the slave:
'Why do you play such awful music?
Don't you ever think? I'll have you whipped
for upsetting your master.'

He does his best to calm the storm.
Wiping his eyes on the sleeve of his gown,
he makes light of the incident.
He contrives a kind of smile.

Drops from the dragon clock[29] announce
that it is one in the morning.
The wife reflects her husband's smile.
She thinks: 'This balances the pain I felt.'

But he feels belittled by his own shame
and is choked with anger.
In his own heart now he tends
a worsening wound.

The married couple go to bed,
to share their loving pillow.

Kiều stays awake all night, huddled by her lamp.
She thinks: 'Now that she has revealed her face,
I can see how it is scarred with bitterness.
And all her machinations were designed
to torture a pair of kingfishers.
She has placed us at opposite poles:
I am the gutter while he is the sky.
Her hand is light as cork,
but heavy as lead.
How can I break free?
I am drowning in her storm,
and the waves of her sea are so strong.'

The lamp sputters and dies,
but her tears continue to flow
beyond the final watch.

*

Kiều serves at the house day and night.
One day, the mistress asks her how she is feeling.
She chooses her words carefully:
'Sometimes I grieve my own destiny.'

Hoạn tells her husband to question Slave Flower:
'Find out what is happening in her head.'

The very idea causes him pain,
as if Hoạn has skewered his gut.
He can neither confess nor look at his beloved.
But if he does not do what she asks,
it is Kiều who will suffer.

Softly he asks Kiều what she thinks about her life.
She does not utter a word.
Instead, still kneeling on the floor,
she begins to write.

She presents him with a sheet of paper
which he hands directly to his wife.

As Hoạn reads, she feels as if
a shoal of silver fish
has flitted across her heart.

'She knows how to write,' she says.
'We should feel for her fate and her suffering.
Had she been born into a luckier existence
she might have been living by now in a golden palace.
Instead, she is a woman adrift in a harsh sea:
blessed with talent, cursed by fate.'

'Now you are telling the truth,' says her husband.
'Cruel fate heaps misery on the finest roses:
this has been a rule of life for centuries.
So be more gentle with her. Treat her kindly.'

Hoạn answers, 'In her poem, she explains
how she would like to pass
through the Gate of Emptiness.
I can help her to achieve that wish.
There is a Buddhist temple in the grounds
dedicated to She Who Listens to the World's Laments.
Its garden contains a four-season lotus
and a hundred-foot tree,
with many plants, flowers and rock pools.
Slave Flower may tend the shrine there.'

*

The sun is rising in a clear sky as they bring the five offerings:
incense, candles, flowers, tea and fruit.
At the altar of Buddha, Kiều makes three vows:
obedience to the Buddha, to the Law and to the Community.
She rejects also the five forbidden things:
promising that she will not harm anything that lives;
that she will not steal;
that she will not fornicate;
that she will not tell lies;
and that she will drink no alcohol
nor chew any herb that changes how the mind works.
She exchanges the blue gown of a slave
for the brown habit of a nun.
She is given a new name: Pure Springwater.
Her task is to refill the oil lamps at dawn and dusk
with two other altar girls: Spring and Autumn.

And so she lives in that grove of purple bamboo,
far from the world's red dust.
Why wait for a love that no longer exists?
She does not have to sell her body.
She buries her sorrow at Buddha's feet.
She copies out the sacred texts by day:
by night, she lights candles and incense.
Holy water sprinkled from that willow
can douse the fires of sinfulness
and wash away the grime of our filthy world.

*

The moon has brightened the garden many times
since first she took the brown habit.
She exists behind the meshed screens
and bolted doors of a Buddhist convent.
When others are present, she smiles;
when she is alone, she weeps.

Thúc's study looks out to her temple,
though in truth they are worlds apart.
One day, while he is idling about his room,
his wife announces that she is leaving
to visit her parents.

Thúc seizes the opportunity. He slips away
and into the garden, and on to the shrine
to meet his love. Finding her, he weeps,
and wipes his tears with the sleeve of his gown.

He says: 'I was the Lord of Spring;
I let my flower be punished alone.
I was outmanoeuvred by my own wife.
I watched what happened to you
but was too dumbstruck to speak out.
It is all my fault that the jade
was trampled into the mud,
that your own spring days have come to such an end.
Yet still I would walk through fire for you,
I would brave the greatest danger –
except that I owe my parents a grandson,
and for their sake alone I must grit my teeth
and sever the knot that binds us.
I let the stone break. I let the bronze fade.
In my next hundred lives I can never atone
for this single promise broken.'

Kiều answers: 'A boat made of cypress wood
will float or capsize as destiny decides.
When I first plunged into this swamp, I never dreamed
that I would ever see you again.
I am a raindrop and I fall
wherever the wind takes me.
But you and I once played the lute,
we plucked those strings

for a few memorable days at least.
If you can find me a way out of this prison,
you will prove your love
and earn my gratitude.'

'I have often thought of helping you that way,' says Thúc,
'for my wife's heart is a bottomless abyss
and I fear that, when her storm breaks,
it will destroy you and cause me terrible grief.
Why not just run away,
flit off into the forgetful night?
You and I walk contrary paths
and perhaps we will never again make vows
for the rivers and mountains to hear.
But those rivers will become desert trails
and those mountains will disintegrate
before this silkworm will forget its cocoon.'

They speak of the past and the future
and keep repeating the same tender words
as if they have an ocean of them.
They hold hands and gaze into each other's eyes
and they find it hard to say goodbye –
until a housemaid gives them a warning sign.
They blush and separate. Thúc starts to leave.
Suddenly Hoạn appears out of nowhere,
brushing away the flowers that had hidden her.

She greets her husband with honeyed smiles:
'Fancy meeting you here. Are you taking a stroll?'

He stammers an excuse. 'I was picking flowers.
Then I decided to drop into the temple
to watch this nun making copies of the scriptures.'

Hoạn praises the brushwork: 'She has such style,
her calligraphy can match the *Lanting Xu* itself.[30]
Such a tragedy that she has been tossed in a river.
Her work would be worth a thousand gold pieces.'

They drink a cup of contemplative apricot tea
and then, arm-in-arm, return to their study.

Kiều feels sad and confused.
She goes to the housemaid
and in an urgent whisper
questions her about what has happened.

'The lady was here for a long time,' says the maid.
'She approached silently, and then hid
for maybe half an hour. She heard
every word that the two of you said:
your troubles, your love for one another,
the master's grief, your wanting to escape.
She made me wait in the corner.
Then, once she had heard everything,
she stepped up to this veranda.'

Kiều's blood runs cold. She thinks:
'That woman is hard to understand.
The coolness of her, the self-control:
just thinking of it sends a shiver down my spine.
She might be the finest actress of her generation.
And Thúc stands there with his arms folded:
another woman would have torn him limb from limb.
She doesn't even raise an eyebrow.
She greets him with laughter and pleasant words.
A furious face tells what's in the heart,
but those who smile and hone their hate
are the ones we should fear the most.

'I need to take charge of my own life.
I must escape the tiger's jaws
and the hidden snake.
If I do not learn to fly, one day
she'll bring her pruning shears to me.
I am a broken fern on a swollen stream:
I never care where the current takes me.
I am lost and alone in a foreign land.
I cannot face the cold with empty hands.'

She looks around and sees the gold and silver
on the altar. She scoops up a couple of pieces
and hides them in her gown.

When the drum sounds for the third watch,
Kiều slips over the temple wall.
She heads west, towards the setting moon.

năm

nam: south; or man
nậm: a small wine bottle
nạm: a handful
nắm: to seize
nám: burnt
nằm: to lie down
nấm: mushroom
năm: five

5

Mist swirls across the sand, towards a wooded hill.
Cocks crow from moonlit huts; she presses
fresh shoeprints onto a dew-soaked bridge.
Through the dawn and the sharp wind, the lone girl walks.

The sun rises over a mulberry orchard:
Kiều wonders where she might find a bed.
Across the field is a Buddhist temple
whose sign reads: 'The Peaceful Haven'.
Kiều walks straight to its gate and knocks.
A little nun scurries out to greet her.

Kiều is dressed in the brown habit of a novice.
Giác Duyên, the Superior, likes the look of her
and asks for her story, from heel to hair.

Kiều is too ashamed to tell the truth.
She claims: 'I am a simple nun from Beijing.
I professed my vows a little while ago.
My superior will explain more when she arrives.
She asked me to bring you these gifts in advance.'

She holds out the items she has taken from the altar:
a golden bell and a silver gong.
Giác Duyên looks at the gifts and says:
'These must be from my old friend, Hằng Thủy.
But it is dangerous for a young novice to be travelling alone:
you must stay here a while to wait for her.'

Kiều joins that community in the clouds
for peaceful days of boiled rice and salted greens.
They chant the old remembered psalms.
Kiều tends the incense

and tidies the nuns' cells.
She hoists the triple banderoles,
giving flight to body, mind and language.
At dusk she lights the lanterns
and snuffs them again at dawn.
Giác Duyên admires how her mind works.
The young nun seems destined for nirvana.

*

Spring is coming to an end.
Petals are strewn across the temple lawns:
by night, a sparkling river seeps across the sky.
Not a breath of wind troubles those peaceful days:
not a cloud, not a sign of discontent.

A pilgrim recognizes two pieces on the altar:
'They look like the ones that were recently stolen
from the temple on Lady Hoạn's estate.'

Giác Duyên finds this observation troubling.
In the dark and silent night, she asks Kiều
to explain her story once again.
So Kiều now tells the truth of her tale
from root through shoot to fallen leaf.
'I am the author of this awfulness,' she admits,
'Whatever happens next is up to you.'

The nun grows pale. She knows how these things work.
She likes the girl, but fears the fist of the law.
In the dead of this night, she whispers to Kiều:
'Buddha's door is open to every sinner,
but I fear those things that I cannot control.
It would wound me if you were captured here.
Think ahead. Run. Don't stand and wait
for the tide to lasso your feet.'

A local family by the name of Bạc
often brings offerings to the temple.
Giác Duyên sends for them and explains
Kiều's difficulties. They agree to shelter the girl
under their own roof.

Kiều accepts without a second thought.
She is desperate to find a home.

*

It presently turns out that Mrs Bạc
has studied at the same school as Mrs Tú.
She is delighted at the natural beauty of the new girl.
It will be easy to turn this into decent profit.
First, she will spin dark tales out of nowhere
to keep the girl obedient with fear.
Next, she will offer her a straight choice:
take a hike along the wild highways
or agree to an honourable marriage
the like of which Châu and Trần might envy.

'You are alone, ten thousand miles from home.
They say good news hangs around
while bad news goes wandering,
but your filthy reputation has done both.
You carry a curse, you mongrel,
you've dragged badness through our home.
There's none but us would take you in.

'Here's what you must do. Either jump
at the first chance of marriage that is offered you,
or find some hole to hide in, in this wild wilderness.
Because there's nobody will marry you round here,
and even further off they can be quite fussy.
But I have a nephew who owes me a favour.

I'll twist his arm. His name is Bạc Hạnh.
He owns a trading store down there in Tiantai.
He'll do for you. He's a decent man.

'After you've married him, you'll live in Tiantai,
where nobody knows you. Think of that – a clean slate,
with new rivers to fish in, new seas to frolic in
to your heart's content. You'll be in your element.
If you refuse, I'll crush you like a beetle.
Disobey me, and I promise you hell.'

Hearing this threat, Kiều knits her brows.
The woman's words fall like blows
from the flat edge of a chopping knife.
The deer stumbled as it ran from the hunt
and now hears the same snarl
from a different set of jaws.
How can she escape?

'I am your servant,' says Kiều. 'I am a lost swallow.
I have been wounded by so many arrows from so many bows
that now I fear the shadow of a bending branch.
If, to escape this current trap,
I am asked to play the wife to a new husband,
how will I know him? How can I read his face?
How might I care for his heart?
And if I am sold to a tiger or a wolf,
then where will I turn?

'If someone loves me, let him tell me,
and let rivers and mountains witness his words.
If someone loves me, let him tell me,
and I will cross the ocean to be at his side.'

The businesswoman translates these words as consent,
and hurries to tell Master Bạc the good news.
Soon the house becomes alive with people:
sweeping the yard, preparing the altar,
cleaning out the wine jars.
Master Bạc kneels to give thanks
to the god of the town and the god of the kitchen.
They make their marriage vows in the backyard
before proceeding to a curtained room
where they tie love's intricate rose-perfumed knot.
Then he escorts her to a boat
and they skip the winds and waves towards Tiantai.

No sooner have they docked
than Master Bạc greets the landlady of his favourite haunt:
a green pavilion, like any other,
a house where flesh is sold or rented out
at a range of competitive prices.
The madam examines the woman Bạc has brought
and makes him an offer
that is ten times more than what he'd spent on her.
Kiều is carried home in a sedan chair,
while he, the well-named, false-faced Bạc,
slinks back to the background that spawned him.

They place her chair at the front door of the brothel,
and a woman comes out to greet her.
This woman welcomes Kiều into the house
and invites her to kneel before the altar of the hairy god.
Kiều understands how such places work:
trapped birds cannot escape their cage.

She says: 'We are cursed,
who are born beneath the peach blossom
and fated to work these green pavilions.
I thought I had escaped them,

but the breeze has blown me back.
To understand life is to know despair.
Genius and beauty are worthless:
they make heaven jealous.
I had filtered my springwater with alum:
it bubbles now with muck and mud.
The potter's wheel torments all women:
it spins and spins, without throwing us off.
When I left home, I accepted my fate:
but why must destiny still hack away
at a rose already shredded?
Half my youth is gone too soon.
I'll offer up the rest of it.
I'll end my young days here.'

                                    *

Cool breeze on a clear night: full moon.
An adventurer from the southern lands
arrives at the bawdy house.
He is a fierce-looking man.
He has the beard of a tiger, a jawbone
as curved and graceful as a swallow's wing.
His eyebrows are rolled as thick as silkworms.
Each shoulder is broad as your forearm is long:
he is a man and a half in height.
He has beaten every enemy with his club or his fist.
He wears heaven like a hat
as he strides about the earth:
he is a free man.
His name is Từ Hải
and he comes from Guangdong.
Over rivers and lakes he wanders,
a sword at his side, a lute at his shoulder,
a single paddle to cross mountains and streams.

He arrives at the entertainment district
to find everyone is talking about Kiều.
The warrior is intrigued by the idea of this girl.
He sends her a message of introduction
and goes to meet her in her rose-perfumed room.
Their eyes meet: their hearts speak.

'And so my heart finds your own at last,' he says.
'Our love is stronger than wind or moonlight.
People tell me how your peach-pink cheeks
are praised by boys you scarcely look at:
but these admirers are not men.
They are fish trapped in pots. They are caged birds.'

Kiều says, 'My Lord, you speak too highly of me.
Who am I to belittle what another might say?
I've mined the chambers of my heart for gold,
but found no one who can bear its lode.
When I greet visitors in this green pavilion,
I have no right to sift a jewel from the grit.'

Từ says: 'How beautifully you speak!
You make me feel like Prince Pingyuan,
who found his finest diplomat
when first he picked a common man.[31]
Come here and look at me. Walk around me.
Is this a man you can trust?'

Kiều says: 'Your heart is mighty and fierce.
One day, greatness will fly over your clouds like a dragon.
When that day comes, this floating weed
might ask you for assistance.'

Từ Hải laughs. He says: 'Not many people can tell who I am,
but your eyes are sharp: you know the world.
You can see a hero through the dust of the road.

When I have ten thousand barrels of rice
and command ten thousand chariots,
I will place you by my side.'

When two souls are destined to be together,
they have no more need for words:
their bodies fit fast and smooth
as two halves of a cleft stone.

Từ Hải goes to the matchmaker,
and pays the owner of the brothel
several hundred liạng for Kiều's release.

He takes her to a bed encrusted with the seven gems –
gold, silver, lapis lazuli, quartz, coral, pearl and amber –
behind curtains embroidered with the eight immortals:
Zhongli Han, whose feather fan brings the dead to life and turns
     stone to gold;
Lü Dongbin, that brilliant drunken poet with his magic sword
     that chases away evil;
Zhang Guolao, old wine-maker, riding his white mule backwards;
Li Tieguai, with his iron crutch and his bottle-gourd stuffed with
     magic potions;
Lan Caihe, half-boy, half-girl, carrying castanets and a flower
     basket;
Cao Guojiu, adviser to the Song, patron saint of drama and the
     stage;
He Xian'gu, with her lotus flower that brings health to all who
     touch it;
and Han Xiangzi, the flutist, with his bouquet of immortal
     peonies.

Từ Hải curves Kiều to him like a phoenix:
she sits astride and rides him like a dragon.

*

After half a year, their love burns brighter than the sun,
but the four winds are calling to his soul.
He stares into the sea and the broad sky,
then chooses a sword and leaps onto his horse.

Kiều says: 'I am a woman, so I must follow.
Take me with you to the limits of the earth.'

Từ says: 'But you know my thoughts exactly –
why play the part of an abandoned woman?
I will return with a hundred thousand men.
My drums will shake the earth.
My banners will cast long shadows on our land
and the world will admire this hero.
Then I will place you by my side and take you home.

'But now I have no home.
If you came with me, you would slow me down,
for I have no place to go.
Wait for me here, where it is safe,
and I will return within the year.'

He spurs his horse and gallops away.
The wind lends him wings upon the long road.
The eagle soars. It hunts across the sky.

*

Kiều sits by the window beneath the plum tree,
and spends her long nights alone behind bolted doors.
The moss in the courtyard springs fresh and untrodden.
The weeds grow wild. The willow grows thin.
Sometimes she gazes into nowhere and imagines
the elms and the catalpas of her parents' backyard.
Clouds drift over the mountains and remind her of home.
She longs to see her own cedar tree, her ageing tiger lily.

Can the passing of time have softened their sadness?
After more than ten years, if they are still alive,
their skin must be wrinkled like walnuts,
their hair must be white as hoar frost.
She dreams also of her lost first love,
whose severed shoot still catches her heart.
She remembers her sister. Suppose Vân married Kim,
and she is cradling his children now, one in each arm.
In exile, Kiều thinks of her distant homeland,
till her thoughts are meshed with misery.
The wild goose has flown beyond the rim of the earth
and she watches the horizon for his return.
She spends her days in silence, her nights in sorrow.

                              *

War comes to the region. Villages are set alight.
Death is in the air, and the scent of burning
drifts on the breeze. Pirates maraud the rivers;
armed soldiers patrol the roads.
Kiều's friends and neighbours urge her to flee.
She tells them: 'I promised Từ Hải I would stay here.
Danger holds no fear for me. I will keep my word.'

Less certain than her words suggest, she waits alone.
Gongs clang. She steps outside. Warriors surround the house,
their scarlet flags fluttering in the breeze.
An armoured officer says: 'We are looking for our Lady.'

They lay down their weapons and kowtow before her.
Ladies-in-waiting approach her. One of them says:
'His Majesty has sent us to your Highness.
We have been commanded to lead you to your husband.'

The carriage is decorated with the sign of the phoenix:
the she-bird that rose from the ashes of its own destruction.
A phoenix is painted on each door and wall,
and each curtain is embroidered with a phoenix.

The soldiers beat the drums, they raise the flags,
they begin the jubilant procession.
Musicians beat a tattoo to the clatter of the wheels
and a crier shouts the good news from his golden tablet.
Their rhythm is answered by rebel drums
from the hills and mountains of the revolutionary south,
for Từ Hải is the new Lord of the southern people.

As they approach his citadel, a cannon sounds.
Defiant flags flutter from the ramparts.
Từ Hải himself comes out to greet them,
swathed in the robes and turban of a warrior chief.
She sees again those heroic features
that once she perceived through the dust of the road.

'You are fish. I am water,' he says.
'Come and swim in me again.
Heroes recognize each other through the blackest filth.
Tell me, is this how you foresaw it would happen?'

She says, 'I am only a vine.
I happened to cling to the strongest tree,
and now I admire the might of his victory.
I sensed your destiny when first we met.'

They gaze into each other's eyes. They smile. They laugh.
They retire to a flower-scented tent
where they tell each other loving secrets.

A banquet is laid out for the honest troops.
The war drums thump and thud.
Rebel songs ring out into the night.

It is good that Kiều should enjoy such moments
after so many years of misery.
And their love grows even stronger
as the fine days slip away.

*

At camp, one day at a quiet hour,
Kiều recounts the tragedy of her past.
She speaks of the residents of Wuxi and of Linzi,
the compassionate and also the treacherous.

She says: 'At last my soul is at peace,
except that I lack two things:
to thank those who were kind to me;
to bring justice to those who did me wrong.'

His thoughts are swift as lightning, and his words
are terrible as the thunder that follows the lightning.
Từ Hải calls his men and chooses the best as captains.
He sends them on their mission under the red flag:
they must run faster than the stars.
One squadron will head for Wuxi and another to Linzi.
They will find the quislings and the traitors,
run them to ground and bring them to trial.
A special agent is sent to ensure that Thúc
and his father are protected from all harm.
Another carries invitations to the nun Giác Duyên,
and to the palace housekeeper who works for the Hoạn family.
Kiều explains again her heartbreak to the soldiers,
whose rage boils over. They scream. They swear revenge.

*

Heaven's vengeance is swift and precise.
The criminals are rounded up. Back at the camp,
soldiers guard them with sharp swords and thick cudgels.
Captured weapons are presented on the ground.
The air falls dark with the shadows of rebel flags.

Từ Hải and his wife take their places at a central tent.
A dreadful drum roll resounds, its thunder still rumbling
as a guard brings the prisoners before them.

Từ Hải says: 'Thank the good; wreak vengeance on the rest.
That is my advice. The power of justice is entirely in your hands.'

She says: 'Whatever power I have, I have borrowed from you.
I will give goodness to those who showed me goodness,
and punishment to those who deserve it.'

He answers: 'My men will follow your orders.'

The first to appear before them is Thúc,
stumbling along at the point of a sword.
His shivers and his sweat tell the story of his past
as starkly as if it were written in indigo.

Kiều says: 'What I owe you is heavier than the mountains.
Do you remember me, who loved you at Linzi?
But night stars can never shine at midday,
nor could we keep those vows that said, "I will follow."
And so I reward you with one hundred rolls of embroidered cloth
and one hundred bags of silver.
But your wife will hear a different story,
because she is a demon.
And now she is trapped, like the unfortunate thief
who broke into the house of the cunning old woman.
The ant is crawling on the inside of my cup:
she does not have long to wait.'

Thúc's face runs with sweat
as if he has been caught in a rainstorm.
He is fearful for one wife and joyful for the other.

The next to be brought are the compassionate housekeeper
from Lady Hoạn's palace and the elderly nun.
Kiều leads them both by the hand to a place of honour.
She removes her veil and says: 'Look.
I am Slave Flower. I am Pure Springwater.
And when I stumbled, you picked me up.
A mountain of gold could not repay your kindness.
But when a washerwoman helped the warrior Han Xin,
he later matched her rice bowl with a bowlful of gold.[32]
I link our story with theirs. I award you a bowlful of gold.'

The two women are astounded.
They stare at her with awe and delight.

She tells them: 'Please, remain in your seats.
Now I will show you the shape of revenge.'

She commands the captains to bring more prisoners.
One draws his sword under the bold red flag
and utters the name of the worst villain: Lady Hoạn.

Kiều greets her: 'My lady, how kind of you to join us.
Few have your calmness or far-sightedness –
nor a heart of such polished granite.
And yet all women should treat others with compassion:
who sows sour seeds will reap a bitter harvest.'

Hoạn sways and stumbles under the shade of that rebel tent.
She admits: 'It's true. I am a woman. I have a heart and a soul.
But what person walks this earth who is free of jealousy?
Remember how I heard and loved your poetry.
Remember how I let you tend the altar at my shrine.

Remember how I sent no guards to prevent your escape.
In the closeness of my heart, I admired you.
Yet where is the woman who likes to share her husband?
I strewed thorns along your path. Forgive me.
Let the level seas wash over my footprints.'

Kiều praises her: 'Your wit is keen as a blade.
You have found the right words.
It would be a mean spirit who would punish you now.
Since you are truly sorry for your misdeeds,
we will leave the past to silence.'

She gives orders for Hoạn to be released.
The lady falls to the floor in gratitude.

Now a long chain of prisoners crosses the gate.
Kiều says: 'The mighty sky that swirls over us all
has noted your wickedness
and now watches your punishment.'

The villains are paraded in reverse chronological order:
Master Bạc and Mrs Bạc; then Sparrowhawk and Dog;
and finally Auntie Tú, with Mã, the college graduate.
They can hardly deny it: they are guilty as charged.
The executioner is ordered to go about his work.
Even the spectators are terrified. He swings his blade.
Gobbets of flesh swish through the air:
heaven's wish sees selfishness is punished.
The wicked are matched with wickedness.
The soldiers crowd around the place of execution
to learn how darkness is extinguished
by the honest light of day.

When Kiều has worked these acts of vengeance,
Giác Duyên asks if she might be allowed to leave.

Kiều says: 'You are a friend of such kindness
that I may meet you only once every thousand years.
Your cloud must drift away from this water fern
to wend its lonely way among the mountain tops.'

The nun says: 'Our future is not what you imagine.
We will meet again within five years.
I met with Tam Hợp, a nun who can see what is to come.
She foretold that I would meet you here – she was right –
and that five years later I would meet you again.
Our friendship will be renewed quite soon.
We will not have to wait a thousand years.'

Kiều says: 'If Tam Hợp remembers the future,
then she knows what happens next.
If you should meet her again, on your winding path,
ask her to tell you the rest of my story.'

Gladly Giác Duyên agrees to this request,
then begins the long road home, towards her distant hills.

*

Now Kiều is happy. She has paired goodness
with goodness, brought badness to the bad.
She kneels at the feet of Từ Hải.

She tells him: 'This weak willow has seen a day
it dared not dream of. And it was you
who threw the thunderbolts that destroyed my enemies
and lifted all the sadness from my heart.
My gratitude is written on my bones.
It will outlive me. They will find it in my grave.'

Từ answers: 'A hero-man does not always find
a hero-woman. This century was lucky.
But when a hero meets villains on the road,
he does not flinch and turn away.
You are my wife. Your sadness is mine.
You must not kneel to thank me.
You told me of your parents:
it is wrong that they must live in the northern capital
while you are queen of the South.
I will never rest until I see you reunited.'

He orders a special banquet for all his troops
to celebrate the triumph of rightness over wrong.

*

When bamboo splits, the whole stem cleaves:
when one tile falls, the roof caves in.
That is how the army of Từ Hải spreads over the land –
finding the fault line in the slate
and striking it precisely.

He calls the sky his homeland
and sets up government
in one corner of it.
His word is counted law
in half the territory of China;
then his armies sweep south
over the five provinces of Nam.

He swings his sword through the harsh wind
and hones it in the swirling dust of combat.
He despises those men whose only work
is to be clothes hangers and boxes for rice.

At last he is master of the wild frontier.
Every warlord, every gang leader must bow to him.
They bend their knee at the sight of his flag.
For five years, he alone is ruler
of all that vast country,
from the mountains down to the coast.

*

But then there arrives a new governor,
whose name is Hu Zongxian.[33]
When he set out from court, the emperor himself
pushed the chariot.

His task is to regain control
over the rebel counties of the south.

Hu Zongxian knows the brilliance of Từ Hải
and knows that he listens to a single voice:
the song of Kiều.

He stations the imperial army at the frontier
and sends an envoy to sue for peace.
This messenger brings gifts of gold and jade and silk,
two handmaids for the Lady Kiều
and a perfumed invitation for Từ Hải:
he should present himself at the imperial court.

Từ Hải receives this offer in his own tent.
Doubts begin to gnaw at his mind
like rats at the millet. He thinks:
'I built this country myself, with these two hands.
I can sail to sea from Chuhe and wade the river at Wujiang.
But at the emperor's court I'd have no more freedom
than does a convict. It would be an act of surrender.
I've seen how these dukes and high-born fools

are caught up in each other's skirts and robes.
They fear my armies. They dare not attack me.
I stride the earth a free man,
with nothing higher than my head, except the sky.'

But Kiều has always trusted people. Even now,
she hears only goodness in the fine words of the messenger.
She thinks: 'I am a floating water fern,
caught up in these quick currents for too long.
Perhaps it is time to end my wandering.
If we swear allegiance to the emperor,
who knows what he will give us in return?
Từ Hải may be made a prince, while I
could return to my parents' house
at the side of my proud husband.
I will be loyal to my parents,
and to the emperor also.
I will no longer be a cypress boat
that floats or sinks at the wish of the waves.'

When they discuss what road to take,
she explains her ideas to him like this:
'The emperor is generous as the rain.
His law keeps the northlands peaceful,
and all his subjects are thankful to him.
But where there is war, the bones of the dead
pile up high. The rivers keep changing their course.
Is that how your people must remember you?
Nobody now praises Hoàng Sào
for leading a failed rebellion a thousand years ago.[34]
Accept the emperor's offer. Take his money.
There is no surer path to nobility and wealth.'

He listens to her words. He hears their wisdom.
He sends out word that the fighting is over.
He loads the envoy high with gifts
and promises to lay down his arms.

Từ Hải keeps his side of the bargain.
The red flag is lowered. The rebel drums are silenced.
The emperor's spies report this weakening of his power.

Hu Zongxian responds with the flag of friendship
which he sends directly to Từ Hải's tent.
Before the flag: another set of gifts.
Behind it: warriors armed to the teeth.

Từ Hải suspects nothing. He rises
to welcome this latest peace offering.
And that is the signal:
the emperor's flags unfurl. Muskets open fire.
The wiliest tiger is caught.

A trapped tiger knows only one destiny:
to die, defeated and distraught.
He fights to the end. He shows them
the strength of a free man's heart.
As his soul leaves this world, his body yet stands
strong as a bronze statue that can never be toppled.

The earth trembles. The beaten run.
The stink of death rises to heaven.
The battlements are torn down.

Escaping rebels bring the news to Kiều.
She runs to the battlefield, where Từ Hải's corpse stands
firm as a mountain, and still unmoved.
She falls at his feet. She says:
'You had a brave heart and a quick mind
until you listened to my advice.
I have no right to look at you.
Let me die here, this same day.'

Her tears flow, the dam has burst,
and she lies prostrate before him.
But here's the strangest thing that happened:
the moment she lies flat, his body keels over.
He falls alongside her.

Some imperial soldiers take pity on her.
They haul her to her feet and revive her.
They escort her back to their own headquarters,
where Hu Zongxian speaks kindly to her:
'Woman, you are weak and vulnerable,
and you were caught up in the crossfire of this war.
We devised our strategy in the command room,
but it was you that carried it out.
You spoke the words that we needed you to say.
You spiked the traitor's guns.
Now that victory is ours, name your price.
I will reward you.'

Kiều's tears fall again: pearls that speak.
And then she says: 'I loved him.
He strode about the earth under the wide sky:
oceans were like streams to him.
His only mistake was listening to me.
He laid his undefeated sword aside
to please his wife.
And now he is gone. Everything ended in a moment.
For five years, no one could challenge him:
but now they dump his carcass in a field.

'You ask what I want for my reward.
Even your praise burns me like fire.
I destroyed him. Why am I alive?
Give me nothing except a little ditch
where I might bury the man I loved in life
and love him still in death.'

Hu Zongxian is moved by her words.
He gives orders to his men.
Từ Hải's corpse is wrapped in grass
and buried by the riverside.

*

The imperial army holds a victory feast.
Strings twang, pipes toot: drinking songs.
Hu Zongxian orders Kiều to serve him with wine.
Half-cut, he picks up a lute and tells her to play it.

Like the whoop of the wind and the lilt of the rain
the lute mourns all those who are dead
and those who live in misery.
Five fingers touch those four strings
as if dripping blood upon them.
Not the howl of a baboon
nor the complaints of the cicadas
could match that song for sadness.

Hu Zongxian frowns, and then he weeps.
He asks: 'What do you call that song?
All the world's grief in a single lament.'

'This song is known as "Cruel Fate",' she says.
'I wrote it long ago, when I was young.
And now I have lived the very sadness
that my song predicts.'

He listens. He is bewitched. He falls in love.
That iron face now falters as he looks at her.
'Let fire and incense witness my vows of love
in this life, through the next life,
into the one after that,' he says.
'Perhaps my phoenix-glue can mend the strings of your lute.'

'I am nobody. I am a woman,' says Kiều.
'And through my fault an honest man is dead.
This flower is starting to fade.
The lute strings of my heart are already snapped.
The only thing I ask is to see once more
the elms of my home village.'

'It will be done,' he says.

Hu Zongxian was drunk when he made his offer,
but he sobers once the sun comes up.
He thinks: 'I am a great man,
an officer in the imperial court,
and I have just won a great victory.
The people look up to me.
The emperor watches me also.
My days of playing at love are gone:
I must get out of this affair.'

As soon as his office opens for business,
he takes the decision coldly.
Nobody can argue with a mandarin.
He arranges for Kiều to marry a local chieftain.

Now, gods, explain yourselves.
Why make these random links between men and women?
Where is the sense or the use of them?
Kiều takes another carriage to another wedding bed.
New curtains are lowered. Fresh candles are lit.

*

Alone, the willow is weeping.
Again, the peach blossom is wet with rain.
And not a spark of youth or happiness is left.
Let the sands bury her, the waves wash over her.

Let her parents forget they ever loved this daughter.
Her talents bring her no joy.
Let her be carried like a sea wrack to a distant coast
where her bones might find a place to rest.

'Who cut the threads of my first love?
Why am I stooped with sadness?
Each day that I live is a wasted day.
To end a life of endless misery
means there is nothing to mourn.
I have decided. The final hour has come
for this skin of ivory, this hair of jade.
The time has come to end it now.'

The moon sinks beyond the western hills.
She walks down to the river's edge
and listens to the fierce roar of its torrents.
She asks a passer-by for the name of the water
and is told: 'This is the Qiantang river.'

This is the place Đạm Tiên once mentioned
when she soothed her in that dream in the brothel
after Kiều had tried to stab herself to death.

She says: 'I have found the right place to die.
Đạm Tiên, my sister, I have kept our appointment.
I know you are waiting for me down below.'

She goes back to her room and writes by lamplight
one last poem: a final testament.
Then she parts the beaded curtain and looks out
over the vast sky and the roaring river
blended by the dark into a single colour.

She thinks: 'Từ Hải trusted me completely
and I betrayed him. I delivered him to the emperor.
I killed my man and now I have another.
How dare I walk about this earth?
I will end this tragedy now.
I put my faith in the wild waves and the sky.'

She finds a steep gorge where there is no shore
and throws herself headlong into the tumult.
Her chieftain husband rushes out to save her,
but the perfumed jade is gone.

*

And that is the cruelty of fate.
Kiều was a woman, with human weaknesses,
but cursed also with good looks and so many talents
that dragged her down to this disgrace.
For fifteen years, she was the perfect model
that other girls would seek to imitate:
now she meets the worst destiny of all.

But she forgot how the world turns.
When yin is gone, yang returns.
Though the best be snarled in misery
heaven will smile, eventually.

sáu

sau: behind
sầu: melancholy
sâu: to decay
sáo: stereotyped and trite (adj.)
sáo: short bamboo blinds (n.)
sấu: the dracontomelum (a
Vietnamese walnut tree)
sáu: six

6

Since leaving Kiều, with a gourd full of water,
Giác Duyên has trudged her mountain path through the clouds.
She visits Tam Hợp, and as they share a cup together
she asks the wise one what will happen to Kiều.

'She has been such a good friend – a loyal daughter and a
      faithful lover –
but she keeps meeting with misfortune,' Giác explains.

'That's how the world is,' says the other.
'The good must suffer; the innocent are punished.
But we are the ones who make the world like that.
Our destiny begins within ourselves. We shape it.
If you don't want the agonies of passionate love, become a nun:
all other roads lead to torment.
Kiều is lucky to be clever and wise,
but unlucky to be beautiful with it.
Those rosy cheeks, that pear blossom:
that's what brings her trouble.
Her other problem is, she can't leave well alone.
She is restless. She gets fired up with passion.
That's why she never stays in one place for too long.
There is a demon on her path and he keeps luring her back to
      misery.
So she follows him, because she is obliged to wander:
that's how destiny works.
One misery ends, to be replaced with another.
Twice she worked those green pavilions;
twice she wore the blue clothes of a servant.

'Here's what happens next. She is happy now,
with her charming bandit, but it will end.
I see her now with other soldiers

and their swords and spears,
at a drunken feast.
She will serve them drinks.
She will play the lute again
to amuse another tyrant.
And she will be hurt again
and feel unutterable loneliness.
And she will throw herself into a fast-moving river
like a fish leaping into a dragon's jaws.
It will not be right, nor just,
but she will do it all the same.
She alone knows why she chooses
to do the things she chooses to do.
She is passionate, and misery loves the passionate,
and misery will love her to the end.
She can never be happy in this lifetime.
Maybe the next.'

Giác Duyên blanches at this dreadful news.
'The next lifetime!' she says.
'But what will become of her in this?'

'There is always room for hope,' says Tam Hợp.
'That tussle with the river need not kill her.
Everything in nature finds a balance,
even the many shortcomings of Kiều.
For example, she loves without thinking:
that is stupid, but it is not unbridled lust.
And while still in love with her first love,
she sold herself to settle her father's debts:
heaven admired her faithfulness there.
Her well-meant advice led to her lover's death:
but that action also saved ten thousand lives.
She can tell right from wrong.
She has done enough good deeds
to outweigh the sins of the past.

Sometimes heaven smiles on those who deserve it.
Giác Duyên, you must go to the Qiantang river
and station a raft along a certain stretch:
thus you will keep your promise to the girl.
As nuns, our work is to bring happiness from heaven.'

Giác Duyên rejoices at this good news.
She journeys to the Qiantang river,
to the place Tam Hợp specified.
She builds herself a hermitage of dried grass and bent willow.
The waves are her emeralds, the clouds her gold.

For several months, she hires two fishermen
to station their boats at either bank of the Qiantang.
They stretch a strong net between them.
She is a woman of great faith. She waits for the great event
that is written in her destiny.

*

When Kiều dives headlong into those silver waters,
she is sucked under by the current,
and then tangled in a net.
The two fishermen pull her to the surface.
They haul her into one of their boats.
Tam Hợp's prediction was perfect.

She lies unconscious on the deck
in her sodden nightdress.
Giác Duyên knows her face at once,
but those eyes are closed. She is in another place.

Kiều is dreaming of plum trees.
Đạm Tiên appears and says:
'My sister, I have been waiting for you
for ten years, haunting this bend of the river.

How fragile is your fate –
but how marvellous your actions!
None can match your goodness. Despite your sins,
heaven loves you. You sold yourself
because you loved your parents.
You did everything to make others happy.
Your goodness at last makes the pendulum reverse.
I cross out your name from the list of the Company of Sadness.
I give you back your poems.
They are the finest in our literature.
Your future now is different.
You will meet again your first love.
You will know happiness.'

While Kiều tries to make sense of this dream,
a soft voice murmurs at her ear: 'Pure Springwater!'
She stirs. She wakes. Two fishermen are leaning over her.
She does not know them. The boat is strange too.
And then she finds Giác Duyên by her side.

The two women brim over with love and happiness.
Kiều revives. Giác Duyên pays the fishermen.

*

Kiều joins the nun in her grass-and-willow hut.
They enjoy the wind and the moonlight,
and they eat boiled rice and salted greens.
They contemplate the vastness that surrounds them,
the rising and the falling of the tides,
the soft clouds at sunrise and sunset.

Đạm Tiên had told her plainly
that she would meet her first love again.
But how will he ever find her here?

*

While Kiều was living through her misery,
young Kim was having troubles of his own:
six months to sort out his uncle's funeral
in faraway Liaoyang.

He returns to Birdwatchers' Paradise expecting to find her,
but everything has changed.
The Vươngs' house is empty, its garden overgrown.
Its windows are silent in the moonlight.
Its walls are lashed with wind and rain.
She is not there. Nobody is there.
(But the pear blossom still looks lovely
as it trembles in the easterly breeze.)
Swallows flap and flutter through the abandoned house:
weeds on the lawn, moss on the pavements.
The gap in the wall, where they met last year,
is a tangle of thorns and briars.
His heart feels cold and heavy.

A neighbour is passing by. Kim asks him
what happened to the people who used to live here.

'Old Vương got himself into trouble with the law.
Young Kiều sold herself to save him.
The family moved to a cheaper neighbourhood.
Vân sews clothes to make a living.
Quan is working as a scribe.
They do the best they can. Life is never easy.'

This news falls like a thunderbolt from a clear sky.
Kim is shocked. He staggers.

He asks around and finds out where they live,
and makes his way to the Vươngs' new home.

It is a hut, with mud walls and a thatched roof
and a ramshackle bamboo fence pocked with holes.
The front door is a threadbare curtain of reeds.
The yard is a patch of weeds dripping with rain.
The very sight of it makes him sadder yet.

He calls out, cheerful as he can, through the fence.
Quan greets him, and leads him by the hand into the house.
The old couple emerge from a back room.

They weep uncontrollably as they explain what happened.
'Young man, our family is cursed.
Kiều's chances of happiness are thinner
than a sheet of paper.
She has broken her promise to you.
She had no choice.
Disaster visited this family
and she sold herself to save us.
It broke her heart to leave us,
but even through her tears she told us
again and again of her promises to you.
She begged her sister Vân to take her place
and thus fulfil the promise that she made you.
Her own miseries are endless.
She forsook you in this life
but asks to be your servant in the next,
or the one after that.
We have written her words on our bones.
O Kiều, my love! My daughter!
Why is your fate so cruel?
Your Kim has come home, my child,
but where are you?'

The more they talk, the more upset they grow.
And as he listens, his high hopes wilt and droop
like boiled cabbage. Now he begins to weep.

His face is drenched with tears.
He goes mad from the sadness.
He falls to the ground and faints,
revives and weeps some more.

With Kim so miserable, Mr Vương stops crying
and tries to console him. He says:
'Look, the plank is already nailed to the boat:
what's done is done.
She cannot marry you: she is too unlucky.
You are right to grieve the one you love,
but your own life is golden. Do not spoil it.'

They try a hundred ways to comfort him
but his grief, though calmed, grows stronger yet.
They bring him those old keepsakes of their love:
gold bracelets, an incense jar, a moon-shaped lute.
This sets him off again.
His heart is completely broken.

'This is all my fault,' he says,
'because I had to go away.
I let my water fern be swept downstream.
Our promises were made of stone and gold
and will not be blown away by a gust of bad luck.
She never shared my bed, but she is still my wife.
I will love her in this life, and the next, and the one after that.
Whatever it takes – money, or time, or hard work –
I will not rest till I have found her again.'

He swears that the power of his love is indestructible.
He is weeping as he says goodbye and leaves them.

He travels home and oversees the construction
of a fine cottage in the middle of his flower garden.
Then he brings the Vươngs to come and live with him,

tending them day and night, as if he were their own son,
as attentively as Kiểu herself would have done.

Though his tears sometimes blotch the ink,
he writes for news of her.
He sends his agents all over the country.
He loses count of what he spends
on salaries and resources to bring her home.
Several times he travels to Linqing
where she first went to live as a married woman.
There is no sign of her between the earth and sky.
He longs for her.
His soul is fired in a kiln.
His heart is furrowed by a plough.
The silkworm grows thinner as it spins.
In the winter frosts, he grows weaker still.
He is caught between life and death.
His tears are real. He seeks her in his dreams.

His cedar tree and his tiger lily are afraid
of what his sorrow might make him do.
With swift diplomacy, they arrange for Kim
to marry Kiểu's sister, the lovely Vân.

They choose a lucky day for the wedding.
Everyone says that this beautiful girl
and her talented scholar
make the perfect couple.
Even Kim cheers up a little.
But his heart is broken.

Making love to Vân,
he thinks of Kiểu,
and thinking of her, he weeps
and a knot tightens in his belly.

Sometimes in his study, late at night,
he lights incense in the remembered jar
and strums the moon-shaped lute.
Those same strings make their moans again
and the scent of sandalwood drifts through the blinds,
till he imagines that he hears her footsteps
and the sound of her voice,
and glimpses her gown from the corner of his eye.

Because his promises were made of stone and gold
he knows that he will see her again.

                              *

His days and nights are filled with misery
and every summer turns quickly to autumn.

One spring, Kim and Quan both take the exam
for placement into the civil service
and each achieves excellent grades.
Heaven's gate is thrown open:
flowers are flung as they take the almond path
towards the imperial palace,
and the scent of those flowers wafts as far
as the elms of their home village.

Vương Quan remembers his duties to the past.
He visits old man Zhong and settles his father's debt
in its entirety. Then he marries Zhong's daughter
and their two clans become one.

Kim is rapidly promoted
through the ranks of the Blue Clouds,
but still he pines for Kiều.
He made promises of stone and gold with her,
but now with Vân he treads that golden path

towards the emperor's door.
He prays for his broken water fern
on the swift-flowing current.
With each prize and each new success
he mourns her forced exile.

He is offered the governorship of Linzi.
He takes his little family on that long road,
over those uncountable valleys,
across the innumerable streams.

He manages his work wisely
and spends quiet days listening
to the lilt of the lute
and the call of the cranes.

One spring night, as they sleep
behind curtains patterned with peaches,
Vân dreams of her sister Kiều.
She wakes and tells her husband.

He is excited at the news.
He notes that Linzi and Linqìng
sound very similar.
There may be a sign in that.

When two sisters find each other in dreams,
the meeting is always charged with significance.

*

Next morning, at his office, he asks
if anyone knows the story of Kiều.
An elderly clerk named Đô makes the following report:

'We are going back ten years or more.
I knew her, of course. I knew them all.
I remember first when Mrs Tú
sent her husband Mã to Beijing,
where he purchased a girl called Kiều.
She was a real beauty – you never saw the like.
She played the lute so that your heart swooned.
She wrote extraordinary poetry.
She hated what they had planned for her,
and she fought them – even tried to kill herself.
But they outdid her with their trickery.
They dragged her through the mud till her heart turned numb.

'She was rescued through marriage
to a scholar by the name of Thúc.
But he already had another wife
who was less keen on the idea.
The wife brought Kiều to the city of Wuxi
for the purpose of tormenting her.
Kiều managed to escape that woman's clutches
but, in another twist of cruel fate,
fell into the hands of the Bạcs.
And they sold her on
to another brothel.

'Kiều is a cloud, a broken fern. She drifts about.
But she was rescued by a rebel chief.
He challenged the government and defeated them.
He outwitted the imperial troops time after time.
He made the sky shake.
He stationed one hundred thousand troops
throughout our province of Linzi.
Kiều was at his side. She was able to put right
everything that had gone wrong in her past life.
She gave good things to good people
and made the wicked suffer.

Everyone spoke well of her for that:
the whole province praised her judgement
and called her husband a hero.
But if you want to know that rebel's name,
I suggest you ask the scholar Thúc.'

Kim thanks Đô for his excellent account
and sends a card to Thúc Kỳ Tâm,
requiring his presence at the Lute Hall.
Kim wants answers to two questions:
the name of Kiều's current husband, and his location.

Thúc answers: 'Those were difficult times.
I did ask about the rebel's name
while I was held prisoner in his camp.
His family name is Từ, and he is called Hải.
He fought with gangsters and the government alike.
He first met Kiều while she was living in Tiantai.
His greatness and her charm made for a perfect match.
He made the earth tremble and the sky shake.
But he took his armies and travelled further east:
since then, there has been no word of him.'

Kim has a tale that lacks an ending:
his own heart now is battered by the wind.
'My little leaf, my fern – you were caught in such storms,
and were trampled so deep in the filth of this world!
You were a petal flung on a fast-flowing river,
while I was nowhere to be found.
To remember our old promises, I still keep
your incense jar and the moon-shaped lute,
but there is no soul in its music now;
there is no spark can light that incense.
While you were lost and lonely in your exile,
I grew fat and comfortable.'

He considers resigning his post.
Then he might climb the hills and cross the rivers
and risk his life on battlefields to find her.
But how can we find one bird in the sky,
one fish in the seamless ocean?

And so he waits for news of her.
Some days it is sunny. Sometimes it rains.

*

A letter arrives from the emperor
on rainbow-coloured paper,
bringing instructions for the two young mandarins.
Kim will take over at Nanping;
Vương will be posted to Fuyang.

They load up carriages and horses
and both families set out upon the same road.
People tell them that the rebels have been crushed:
the waters are calm now at Fujian;
the bush fires extinguished at Zhejiang.

Kim fears what this news might mean for Kiều.
He asks Vương to help him search for her.

At Hangzhou, the locals give them this account:
'They ambushed the hero, Từ Hải,
and executed him in a common field,
having first used Kiều to weaken him.
But they gave her no reward;
instead, they married her to a tribal chief.
She drowned herself. Her loveliness
of pearl and jade has found a watery grave
in the Qiantang river.'

So while Kim was enjoying promotions and a comfortable life,
Kiều was driven to suicide. They will never meet again.

*

So that her soul might find some peace,
Kim builds a little shrine at the very bend
of the river where she chose her end.
The waters are wild here. The waves froth.
He imagines how the wing of his wild goose
must have dropped into this tumult.

But our lives are full of mystery.
Who knows what chance brings Giác Duyên
along that river path at just that moment?
She reads the name on the remembrance stone
and greets the mourners at their shrine:
'Who are you? You are friends of mine
if you are family of hers, or if you love her.
Kiều is not dead – take off these mourning clothes!'

They hear these words and their hearts leap.
They surround her and ask a hundred questions
and make hasty introductions:
here is her husband, her parents, her sister,
her brother and his wife.
They had learned of her death from a trustworthy source
so this new notion astounds them.

The nun says: 'Everything that happens is fate.
It was fate that took her to Linzi,
and fate that I found her in the Qiantang river.
She wanted to drown her lovely body,
but I anticipated it. I brought her ashore.
She lives with me now as a Buddhist nun:
our grass-and-willow convent is nearby.

With Buddha, everything is calm.
The days go by.
Yet still her heart is fixed upon her home.'

On hearing this, they laugh
and smile at one another.
The leaf blew from the orchard
and since that gloomy day
they had looked for it in streams
and scanned the skies.
But her rose seemed to have snapped,
its perfume was no more.
They might meet her in the next life,
but had given up hope
of ever finding her in this.
The worlds of dark and daylight
are crossed by very different roads.

But now they learn she has returned
from the Yellow Springs,
they kneel at the feet of Giác Duyên.
They follow as she leads them through the undergrowth.
As they break through the briar and the bracken
they cannot help fearing that this path might lead nowhere.
It is a difficult route, beside that roaring river,
through thick forest, but at last they arrive
at a rustic Buddhist temple.
Giác Duyên calls out the name of Pure Springwater,
and from an inner room
she finally emerges.

At a glance, she recognizes her own family:
the cedar tree is strong, the tiger lily lovely;
Vân and Quan are quite grown up;
and that looks like her first love, Kim –
but this must be a dream.
Such miracles are rarely what they seem.

These tears feel real enough,
and they fall like pearls and stain her dress.
She feels grief mixed with happiness.

She falls at the feet of her tiger lily
and through her sobs confesses her story:
'It is fifteen years since I fell like a broken leaf
into a swift-flowing river.
I tried to end my life by jumping into that cascade.
I never thought I would see you again.'

Her parents hold her by the hand.
Her face has hardly changed since she left home:
the moon a little darker,
the flower battered by the storm.
No scale could make a measure of their happiness.

Her siblings babble with questions and news:
so much to say about the present and the past.
Kim watches and smiles at the three of them;
all his sadness turned to quiet joy.
They kneel before Buddha's altar
and offer thanks that Kiều has returned to life.

They order sedan chairs, decked with flowers.
Vương insists his daughter be carried home with them.

Kiều says: 'I am nothing but a fallen leaf.
For half my life I've lived on bitterness and bile.
I tried to kill myself not long ago
by leaping into those unforgiving waters.
I never dreamed I would see you all again.
But I survived. And we are all together,
and this has quenched the thirst that parched my soul.

'But this convent is now my home.
Here, beneath these trees and in this long grass,
this nunnery holds everything I need.
I eat boiled rice and salted greens;
I wear these simple clothes that a nun must wear.
The passion is gone out of my heart:
why should I crawl back to the world's muck?
Why should I leave my holy work half done?
I am a nun, and I will die a nun.
I owe my life to her who pulled me from the river.
How can I abandon her, and walk away?'

Her father says: 'These are different times.
Holy orders sometimes have to change.
It is good to worship gods and the Buddha –
but where is the girl who'll look after her parents,
the woman who'll cling to her husband?
This gentle nun has saved your life, and so
we'll build a temple in the grounds of our new house.
She can come and live in it, and be near you.'

Kiều hears her father's words and obeys them.
She says goodbye to the convent and to Giác Duyên.

*

The family returns to Kim's own Lute Hall,
where they begin the homecoming feast.
And when the wine has given her the courage,
Vân gets up to speak. She says:
'Heaven decides when lovers meet.
It chose the moment when my sister met my husband.
It witnessed their vows.
But when debt's hurricane destroyed our home,
I took her place. And I was joined to Kim
as a mustard seed is drawn to amber

or a needle to a magnet.
Family is blood, and when blood is spilt
a family must stand together.
For fifteen years we mourned my sister Kiều:
with sadness and with love we longed for her.
But the mirror that was cracked
is clear and smooth again.
The potter's wheel has turned:
it brought her home.
I know she loves him still
and the same moon looks down
that once smiled on their young promises.
Pick the plums while there are still some left.
The peaches are fresh.
It is good to take a bite.'

Kiều answers her sister's words like this:
'Those things happened ten thousand years ago.
Certainly we made vows, but since that day
the wind and rain have battered me.
My past is too shameful to talk about.
Throw it into the river, sweep it out to the sea.'

Kim says: 'These are strange words.
Your feelings may have changed, but our promises do not.
The mountains and the rivers heard them.
The earth and the sky were our witnesses.
People can change – the stars might change their course –
but stone and gold remain through life and death.
It was destiny that brought you back to me:
the two of us are one: why live apart?'

Kiều answers: 'Everyone longs
for a peaceful and a loving home,
and I am no exception.
But I believe a bride should bring her groom

a closed bud, a perfect crescent –
I'm ashamed to think of what I'd bring you.
Cruel fate has had its sport with me
till my flower was swarmed about
by butterflies and bees.
That rain was cold, that wind was hard;
and flowers fade, and the moon wanes.
Look now at my face: these cheeks were roses once.
But life is lived and cannot be unlived.
Can you picture me playing the fair young wife
with a linen skirt and a thorn for a hairpin?
I know you love me, and you kept our promises,
but as soon as our bedroom lamps were lit
there would be no nook to hide my shame.
My bedroom door must stay locked tonight
and every night. I live now like a nun,
though I keep no vows.
So let us love as friends do:
instead of playing duets on our lovers' harp
we'll play a little lute – and then a game of chess.
Don't talk of marriage and its silken knot.
It breaks my heart.'

Kim says: 'How skilful you are with words!
But you forget the many good deeds of your past
that far outweigh whatever guilt you're feeling.
Words like "chastity" have many definitions:
they cannot mean the same thing in peacetime as in war.
You were a loyal daughter, and you did
those things that women have to do:
no dirt would dare to darken you.
Now fate has given us a second chance.
The mists have rolled away. The clouds are gone.
The flower might have faded but it blooms again.
The moon might be waning but it still shines bright.
When Tiêu-lang's wife, Green Pearl, was kidnapped

and given to a general as a prize,
she never looked her husband in the eye again.
She counted him a stranger.
Don't act that way with me.'

He begs. He pleads with her. She listens.
Her parents also speak on his behalf.

At last, there is no more to be said.
She sighs and lowers her eyes.

*

Bright candles for the wedding feast:
a sea of flowers on a red silk rug.
The bride and groom kneel before their parents.
They recite some words. They are man and wife.

In the bedroom, they toast each other's health.
But they are shy of each other now, for all
they might remember stirrings of an old passion.
Fifteen years have passed since the lotus shoot
first touched the perfect peach bud.
Fate made them fall in love,
fate tore them apart,
fate has brought them back together.
There is so much to talk about, this quiet night.

A full moon rises in a clear sky.
It is late. They lower the curtain.
In the lamplight, her cheeks become peaches again.
His face touches her face.
The bee plays around the petals of the flower.

Kiều says: 'I go wherever fate takes me,
but this old body has grown tired now.
I remembered our promises
and I did what you asked:
I acted out the wedding game that everybody needed,
but I felt half ashamed to play my part in it.
There was no truth in those scripted vows.
If we love each other as good friends should,
then I will always love you as a friend.
But if what you want is what all men want,
then take it. Pluck these wilted petals.
And neither of us will ever feel
a passion stronger than contempt.
Love and shame can never mix.
If you are hoping for a child – well,
you have my younger sister.
Why take the only pride I still have left?
I feel such tenderness for you.
Don't spoil it. Don't trample on this flower.'

'What joined us was a single word,'
says Kim, 'and the word was love.
Then we were forced to part:
the fish to the ocean and the bird to the sky.
How I missed you when you were far away!
How it must have hurt you
to break our promises!
But we loved each other:
we looked death in the eye
and we stared it down.
Now we meet again
and we love each other still.
A willow in late spring
has many green leaves:
I thought you might feel a spark for me yet.
But I can see your mirror is perfect now;

it is smooth and whole again.
I did not dredge the ocean to find my pin
because I wanted moonlight and flowers.
My love is made of stone and gold.
We live together, under the same roof:
we do not have to share the same bed.'

Kiều pins back her hair and refastens her gown.
She kneels, and touches her forehead
on the floor before him.

She says: 'If I can ever become myself again,
I will have you to thank for it.
The words you just spoke
prove that your soul and mine are one.
No lovers ever knew a love like ours.
You shelter and protect me. I want no more
from this night. My honour is alive again.'

They let go of each other's hands,
then catch hold of them again.
He loves her now more than he ever did.

He lights another lamp and refills the incense,
which reminds him of something long ago.
He asks her if she still plays the lute.

'Those four strings have brought me too much heartache,'
she says, 'a sadness that continues to this day.
But regrets are useless: they don't change the past.
Because you love me, I will play for you.
I will play a new lament.'

Her fingers dance about the strings
and the scent of sandalwood grows more intense.
Is this the butterfly that dreamed it was Zhuangzi,

or is Zhuangzi dreaming of his wings again?[35]
Is this that king who became every cuckoo
to mourn from every mountainside
the loss of his land and his love?
Clear notes drop like pearls into a moonlit bay
and shimmer like the heat from sun-warmed jade.

He listens to the weave and weft of the five tones
and it thrills his heart.

'But this is the same melody you used to play,' he says.
'It sounds so cheerful now, though it was sad before.
Why does it sound so different?'

'Probably I lacked the skill before,' says Kiêu.
'These fingers on these strings have caused me so much grief.
But now you've heard my little tune
the way it should be played,
I'll put away my lute. That was my final song.'

And they tell each other loving secrets
until the sun-crow rises over the eastern mountains.

*

Kim explains everything about their new arrangement.
Her parents marvel at her wish
and the force of her will.
She is not the kind of girl
to give peaches to one man in the morning
and plums to another at night.

They are in love, and they are friends.
They share no bed, but they write poetry
and sometimes they play the lute.
They might drink wine, or play a game of chess,

or look at flowers, or wait to watch the moonrise.
And everything they wish for comes true
because it is their destiny to be together;
marriage turns these lovers into friends.

And as they promised, they build a temple on a hill
and send an agent to look for Giác Duyên,
but he cannot find her. Her convent is abandoned:
weeds grow wild on the roof, moss fills the cracks in the walls.
The locals explain that she left for a far region,
in search of plants and healing herbs.
And how can we search for a cloud in the sky,
or follow a wandering crane?

In case the old nun might happen to return,
Kiều keeps the temple lit.
She burns candles night and day.

Their home grows happier each year.
Kim rises swiftly through the ranks.
Vân cares for their family, the way a strong tree
bends to shelter young shoots.
Their children grow more talented and wise
than the brilliant sons of Đậu Vũ Quân.[36]

*

Contemplate the lessons of this story:
heaven decides everything. Our destiny is written.
Some suffer dreadful misery;
some live lives of luxury.
The most talented are not always
the ones who succeed:
that would be too neat and is too rare.
Looks and luck don't always rhyme.
Never complain about your fate:

you have one life. Live it.
Within yourself, you hold a precious gift,
worth more than all the talents on this earth:
a human heart.

*

Reader, may these plain but honest words I write
brighten the long hours of your own dark night.

Appendix: An Early Account of the Cuiqiao Story

Here I offer a translation of one of the earliest accounts of Qiao's story as it was told by Xu Xuemo. Xu recorded that he heard the story from many citizens of Haishang, who in turn had heard it from oral accounts by a storyteller called Hua Laoren. It represents perhaps a midway stage in the evolution of the myth, where Quiqiao was no longer the passive concubine she had been in Mao Kun's account, but had not yet become the heroic figure who takes centre stage in *The Song of Kiều*. It will be noted that the essential details of Kiều's biography are beginning to be fleshed out, and also that the narrative is starting to turn against Hu Zongxian:

Wang Quiqiao was a prostitute from Linzi, originally known as Ma Qiao'er because the brothel she had been sold to was run by a woman with the surname Ma. Qiao was famous for composing music and was skilled at playing the lute. She succeeded in escaping from Ma's brothel through trickery, after which she headed south across the sea to Haishang, where she changed her name to Wang Quiqiao.

When pirates attacked the coastal regions south of the Yangtze river, Qiao was captured and was taken to the pirates' lair. Xu Hai, the leader of the pirates, fell in love with her and took her as a wife. He followed her advice in everything. Secretly hoping to return to her own country, Qiao pretended to help him while actually planning to bring about his downfall.

Hu Zongxian, the governor of Zhejiang Province, sent an officer named Hua to summon Xu Hai to surrender. This incensed Xu Hai, who tied up officer Hua and was about to kill him until Qiao interceded.

(Qiao happened to recognize Hua, who came from Haishang.) She said to Xu Hai, 'Look, it's up to you whether or not you surrender, but it is unfair to blame this man who was only carrying the message.' She then untied Hua, gave him money and guaranteed his safety. Hua also recognized Qiao, but fearing for his safety, dared not reveal this.

Returning to the governor's court, Hua reported that Xu Hai had refused to surrender, but that his wife seemed to have a different way of thinking, and she might be of help in bringing the pirate to justice. Hu Zongxian agreed. He sent a second officer, Luo, to negotiate with Xu Hai, along with secret gifts of money, pearls and jade for Qiao. Qiao then began to explain to her husband that the pirates could never win, and that the conflict had already been going on for too long. She suggested that by laying down his arms Xu Hai could take up a role in the imperial government, and that the two of them could thus live comfortable lives in the future. Xu agreed, and sent a message to the government that he was prepared to surrender in return for safe treatment and a government post.

Hu Zongxian sent a message ostensibly accepting these terms of surrender, while secretly preparing an ambush. Trusting Qiao completely, Xu Hai suspected nothing and made no preparations for battle. He walked into the ambush – the army killed him instantly and took Qiao captive. The army chased down and killed all Xu Hai's men and thus achieved a total victory.

Hu rewarded his army with a feast in their camp. He commanded that Qiao must sing and drink alcohol. All his officers stood to toast Hu's health. Hu was happy and drunk. He went down the steps and flirted with Qiao. The banquet continued until late, and Hu spent the whole time with Qiao. The following day, he regretted his dalliance with Qiao, but was reluctant to have her killed, given how important her assistance had been in arranging the capture of Xu Hai. Accordingly he gave Qiao to one of his officers who was about to take up a post in Yongshun. When she was crossing the Qiantang river with this officer by boat, Qiao sighed: 'Xu Hai was faithful to me and I betrayed him by conspiring with the imperial forces. Now a good man is dead and I am betrothed to a stranger. How can I face decent society?'

It was midnight. She threw herself into the turbulent waters.[37]

Notes

1. The famous opening lines of the poem are also the part where this translation has strayed furthest from the original text. The most striking image missing from this English version is that of the *cuộc bể dâu*, which we might translate literally as 'the sea-mulberry game' or more figuratively as 'whirligig' or 'rollercoaster ride'. The intended reference (which would be easily understood in Vietnamese) is to a notion taken from classical poetry, in which every thirty years the sea becomes a mulberry field and the mulberry fields become the sea. In other words, human life involves a constant shifting in fortunes, reminiscent of the idea in Ecclesiastes that 'the race is not to the swift nor the battle to the strong'. The original poem also uses the expression *má hồng* (literally 'rosy cheeks') as a synecdoche for beautiful people.

2. The founder of the Ming dynasty, Zhu Yuanzhang, established his original home-base at Nanjing as the southern capital, with Beijing as the northern capital. (See the Introduction, p. xxi.)

3. The Chinese lunar calendar is divided into twenty-four periods of roughly fifteen days, rather than Europe's twelve periods of roughly thirty. Qingming Day lends its name to the whole period which in our Gregorian calendar coincides with early April. Its name combines the names of the two dynasties whose reversal in fortunes is at the heart of the myth of Kiều (Ming = bright, Qing = pure; see the Introduction, p. xxii). Hanshi (Cold Food Day) occurs a day or two earlier, and the combination of these two days is known as the Tombsweeping Festival, when people traditionally visit their family's graves, take a walk in countryside and play cuju (an ancient Chinese game, similar to football).

4. Along with the Lantern Festival in mid-February, the Tombsweeping Festival was one of only two occasions when middle- and upper-class girls and women were allowed to leave the house. Many romantic

novels open with a description of those days, when talented young men were able at last to meet beautiful women. This is the central motif of the so-called talent-beauty novel, which clearly influences *The Song of Kiều*. (For a fuller description of talent-beauty novels, see the Introduction, pp. xv–xvi.) In some examples of the genre, the man waiting to meet the young women is not a talented young scholar but a wicked villain.

5. Huangquan (黃泉) or 'Yellow Springs' is one of the names of the Chinese underworld – compare the Japanese term 'Yomi'.

6. Women and girls in Ming-era China lived strictly cloistered lives. Well-to-do families lived in walled properties that had two gates – the main gate opened onto the street, while the second gate was inside the estate and led into the back garden, where the women and children lived. Young women were not allowed to step outside this second gate apart from on the days mentioned in notes 3 and 4 above. For that reason, Kiều and her sister seem so far away from Kim, even though he lives just around the corner.

7. 'Red shadows' (*bóng hồng*) is a traditional Vietnamese image for beautiful women seen from a distance.

8. Several philosophies – most obviously Buddhism, Taoism and Confucianism – inform *The Song of Kiều*'s ontological sensibility and its view of the universe, but the afterworld it describes is pretty much unique to itself. Đạm Tiên hints at it here, with this strange register of broken-hearted people who sense a kinship with each other and with Kiều, and who naturally value the craft of poetry above all other human accomplishments.

9. The bird in question is a kingfisher (*thúy*). Kiều's full name is Vương Thúy Kiều.

10. The reference is to two famous female poets of ancient times. Ban Jieyu rose from being a lowly chambermaid to becoming the most favoured consort of the Emperor Cheng of Han (51–7 BCE). In a famous poem attributed to her, she compares herself to a discarded autumn fan. Three hundred years later, Xie Taoyun was the niece of Xie An, the imperial tutor, who asked her to describe what the snow looked like – was it not like a grain of salt? She answered that the colour of salt was good, but snow's shape and behaviour was more like willow catkin swirling in the wind. This combination of salt with catkin became a byword for creative metaphors.

11. All four of these songs have special significance, and for centuries all four have been considered classics. This first reference is to the Battle of Gaixia (202 BCE), fought between Xiang Yu of the Chu and Liu

Bang of the Han. The latter won the battle decisively, leading to the foundation of the Han dynasty (206 BCE–220 CE). The melody mimics the sounds of battle, with its gongs and drums; it also creates a sense of tension when Xiang Yu is surrounded and trapped; it ends with Xiang's sighs and sadness at leaving his lover, as he commits suicide.

12. The second song remembers a troubled love affair between two poets – a penniless young man, Sima Xiangru, who woos a seventeen-year-old widow, Zhuo Wenjun, by singing 'The He-Phoenix seeks the She-Phoenix' (鳳求凰) at her father's house, while she listens from behind a curtain. The wind lifts the curtain; they see each other and fall in love. Her father was opposed to their relationship, and so they eloped to his hometown of Chengdu. Later, when Sima Xiangru travels to the Han capital and finds fame and fortune, he meets many beautiful girls and decides to marry one of them. He writes to Zhuo Wenjun, breaking off with her. In response, she writes one of the most famous of all classical love poems, 'Baitou Yin' ('White-Haired Song'): 'Love is pure as snow and bright as moonlight. So, you've found another woman and you want to say goodbye. Then this is our last poem-party. Tomorrow we'll part by the old canal. I walk along it sadly. The waters flow on. When we married, I never cried about leaving home, like ordinary girls do. I knew you were the one, and I would stay with you though my hair turned white. Love should be pliable and strong as a fishing rod, and lovely and lively as fish. Men should always value loyalty, which is worth more than treasure or gold.' This sparked an exchange of poems between them, at the end of which Sima Xiangru abandoned the idea of staying in the capital and returned home to his first love.

13. One of the oldest Chinese melodies, 'Guangling San' (simply meaning 'Guangling-style music' – Guangling being an old name for Yanzhou, where Marco Polo claimed to have held a senior post) is said to be based on an even older song with the more explicative title, 'Song of Nie Zheng Assassinating the Han King'. Nie Zheng's father was a blacksmith who made swords for the king. Following a delay in a shipment of swords, the king had the blacksmith executed. Nie Zheng vowed to revenge his father's death, but he knew that as a commoner he would find it impossible to get near him. Learning that the king loved music, he retreated to the mountains, where he taught himself to play the qin (a lute-like instrument). Ten years later, he travelled to the environs of the palace, where he played so beautifully that his reputation reached the ears of the king, who summoned him for a

command performance. Once inside the throne room, as the king sat down to listen, Nie Zheng pulled a dagger from inside his qin and stabbed the king to death.

As for the melody, it is said to have originated from a couple of centuries later, from an incident involving the finest musician of his day, Ji Kang (224–263). Ji Kang was playing his qin in Huangyang pagoda in Luoxi, when he noticed that an old man was watching him appraisingly. 'So how am I doing?' Ji Kang asked him. 'Technically you are perfect,' said the old man. 'But you are making that powerful song sound bland and sweet. There is no soul in your playing. Music needs to have feeling.' 'Fine,' said Ji Kang, handing over his qin. 'Let's hear you, then.' The old man picked up the qin and began to play, and suddenly Ji Kang could hear in the same tune the sadness of the assassin, how he missed his father, how his mother loved him, how he had suffered in the mountains while he was learning his craft. Ji Kang knew that this was how music should be played. He asked the old man to teach him: the result was the version of 'Guangling San' that has been passed down to us.

14. The talented Wang Zhaojun was a lowly maid in an emperor's palace. The emperor wanted to marry the most beautiful girl in the kingdom, but there were too many girls for him to meet in person, so he hired an artist to make sketches of them – he would leaf through the sketches, select the prettiest, and then meet the shortlisted girls face-to-face. After several such interview sessions, he still had not found the girl he was looking for. The artist, however, was onto a money-spinner, since the girls would bribe him to paint them prettier, ensuring that they made the shortlist. Wang Zhaojun was too poor, too proud and too honest to bribe him, so he made her the ugliest of the lot. There came a time when the emperor was making a peace treaty with the chief of the Huns, and he offered to throw in five palace girls as a sweetener. To select the girls, the emperor went to the very bottom of his pile of sketches so as to choose the five plainest girls. When Wang Zhaojun was brought forward to cement the deal, the Hun chief was delighted, but the emperor was appalled – this was the girl of his dreams, yet he could not cause a diplomatic incident by recalling her at this stage of the negotiations. Wang Zhaojun therefore found herself sent into exile to the wintry land of the Huns. She was brilliant as well as beautiful – the song that she wrote about crossing the checkpoint to leave China became one of the most famous homesickness songs of all time, and this is the song which Kiều sings here. The incident worked out badly for the artist – the emperor

had him beheaded for making such a bad sketch. It worked out well for the Huns, though – Wang Zhaojun married their chief and stayed there for sixty years, bringing civilization and peace to their nation.

15. I borrowed the expression from Konrad Lorenz (1903–89), the Austrian zoologist and ethologist, who in turn borrowed it from greylag geese. He explains that this is what those geese are honking as skeins of them scud across autumn skies.

16. Cui Yingying and Zhang Sheng were the minister's daughter and the young scholar who eventually succeeded in getting married despite (a) parental disapproval and (b) a bandit chief trying to kidnap Cui Yingying. They are the central characters of the classic drama *Xixiang Ji* (*Romance of the Western Chamber*, 西廂記) by Wang Shifu, which is one of the most significant works praised and annotated by Jin Shengtan. (Jin Shengtan's unwitting role in the development of the Kiều myth is discussed in the Introduction, pp. xxx–xxxiv.)

17. One of the main cities in Manchuria, Liaoyang was the first city the Manchu captured in the 1620s, using it as a base from which to launch their overthrow of the Ming. Its choice as the source of the news that triggers the disaster in *Kiều* is therefore especially significant. (See the map on p. lxvii.)

18. Asian languages tend to treat the gut as the seat of emotions, whereas European languages prefer the heart. Of course there is no biological reason why a digestive organ should be preferred over a circulatory one for this function, nor vice versa, given that the processing of emotions in fact takes place in the brain, probably in the amygdala.

19. The cangue was a kind of portable pillory, made from seasoned wood and weighing between nine and fifteen kilograms, depending on the seriousness of the crime. The intention was to humiliate and to restrict movement – a cangue-wearer usually needed someone else to feed them, as they were unable to reach their mouths with their hands. It took the form of a large square board, split in half and hinged, with two semicircles in the middle of the internal edges for the neck, so that it could be closed and locked, with the head above the cangue and the body below. The effect resembles a living portrait of a head with a thick wooden frame around it, to which are attached labels noting the wearer's name and crime.

20. During the Ming and Qing eras, Linqing was famous for producing the tiles used for building the Great Wall.

21. Ti Ying's father was a country doctor during the reign of Emperor Wen of Han (202–157 BCE), famous for treating the poor as well as

the rich. When one of his wealthier patients died, he was falsely accused of malpractice and sentenced to one of the Five Punishments, which could include amputation or death. His daughter petitioned the emperor, pointing out that such drastic punishments cannot be reversed if the defendant later turns out to be innocent. Impressed by her arguments, the emperor not only pardoned her father but abolished the Five Punishments.

22. The tale is from a collection of supernatural folk stories, *Soushen Ji* ('Looking for Ghosts'), published around 350 CE by the historian Gan Bao. A huge snake, with a head the size of a grain silo and eyes like wall mirrors, was terrorizing a village. It came to the village elders in dreams, telling them that once a year it needed to eat a twelve-year-old girl and demanding that the village provide one. Nine years went by; the snake ate nine young girls. On the tenth year, a girl called Li Ji volunteered to be the next victim. Her parents refused to let her go. Before dawn the next day, she sneaked out of the house, taking her father's sword and a hunting dog, along with some rice cakes soaked with honey, which she placed by the entrance to the snake's cave. When the snake appeared, it headed straight for the rice cakes. As soon as it started eating, Li Ji ordered her dog to attack. When the snake whirled about to attack the dog, the girl stabbed the snake several times in the back of the neck. The snake writhed its way to the temple grounds, where it died. Li Ji strolled home a hero.

23. The green (青) in 'green pavilion' (青樓) sometimes equates to turquoise and sometimes to a deep ultramarine blue. In the Three Kingdoms period (220–280 CE) a green pavilion was simply the term for a mansion, a house associated with money and power. It became fashionable to construct brothels in this colour, by way of making them seem lavish and more salubrious, so that eventually the term 'green pavilion' became a synonym for 'brothel', regardless of the colour of the building.

24. The Qiantang river, which flows through Hangzhou, plays an important role in *The Song of Kiều*. Situated at the southern end of the Grand Canal, it connects to inland waterways that enable waterborne traffic to reach as far north as Beijing. It also has the world's largest tidal bore, its great waves (for centuries known as the notorious Silver Dragon) regularly reaching ten metres in height. Tourists today come to watch the mighty wave from safe vantage points, although in certain conditions the wave can almost double in height, making these vantage points quite perilous. Sightseers are often drenched in water, and in some years the huge wave causes fatalities.

25.   Song Yu was a famous poet from the third century BCE, reputedly
      a womanizer. For Sima Xiangru, see note 12, about the phoenix
      song.

26.   It is said that the city's name comes from an ancient stone found at
      the spot, with an inscription saying: 'Where there is tin, there is an
      army. Where there is an army, there is conflict. Where there is no tin,
      there is peace.' Wuxi (無錫) means 'no tin'.

27.   Chang'e was originally the wife of the legendary archer Hou Yi.
      Long ago, the earth was being scorched by ten suns: Yi shot down
      nine of them, leaving just the one, bringing the temperature down to
      a manageable level. As a reward, he was given the elixir of immortal-
      ity. When he went out hunting, his wicked apprentice tried to steal
      the elixir, and in order to stop him taking it, Chang'e drank it herself.
      This made her immortal, and so she escaped to live by herself on the
      moon. Hou Yi vowed to remember her by eating mooncakes each
      autumn at the Mooncake Festival. China's lunar probes have been
      named after her, just as American probes are named after the Greek
      god Apollo. In January 2019, the Chinese spacecraft Chang'e 4
      became the first lunar probe to explore the far side of the moon.

28.   The Yang Pass traditionally marked the westernmost point of China,
      a fortified mountain pass on the Silk Road. It was traditionally used
      in poetry when referring to sad partings. It also contains the sense
      of being the point of no return.

29.   A dragon clock consisted of a carved wooden dragon whose body
      supported a horizontal lit taper. The taper would burn through cords
      suspending small metal balls, which would then fall, two by two,
      into a brass dish, sounding the passage of time.

30.   The art of calligraphy is still highly prized among Chinese communi-
      ties worldwide. The reference here is to the most famous calligraphic
      work of all time, the *Lanting Ji Xu* (*Preface to the Orchid Pavilion
      Poems*, 蘭亭集序), created by the great Wang Xizhi (303–361). A group
      of poets gathered for a purification ceremony in the year 353 in Shao-
      xing, producing a series of poems as part of a wine-drinking game.
      Xizhi's Preface to their collection proved the most extraordinary
      piece of all, written in a beautiful semi-cursive script and contrasting
      the wonderful vastness of the universe with the fleeting moment of
      human existence. It is said that the original document was later seized
      by an emperor, who had it buried with him; the many versions of the
      Preface still in existence are mere copies of that masterpiece. The
      Preface remains famous throughout East Asia, particularly in Japan,
      where a huge festival to commemorate the *Lanting* poems takes place

in late April, once every sixty years. The twenty-eighth festival will be held in 2033.

31. Prince Pingyuan (平原君, c.308–251 BCE) was the younger brother of the King of Zhao, whose capital Handan was under siege by the Qin towards the end of the Warring States period. His brother asked him to put together an elite band of twenty warriors to accompany him to ask the King of Chu for his help in fighting off the Qin. Pingyuan could find only nineteen suitable men, but a lowly retainer called Mao Sui volunteered for duty. 'How long have you been with me?' asked Pingyuan. 'Three years,' answered Mao Sui. 'If I had put a sharp awl in a leather sack, after three years I'd expect to see a hole. I've never even heard of you. You must be one blunt awl.' 'I'm too low-level for you to have noticed me. I'm asking you to put me in your sack now. If you'd done that years ago, you wouldn't just be seeing a hole – the entire awl would have fallen out.' Impressed with this reply, Prince Pingyuan appointed Mao Sui as one of his elite squad. When they got to Chu, however, Pingyuan was humiliated by the King of Chu, who refused to help and ordered them all to leave. Pingyuan retreated outside to discuss tactics with his advisers. Mao Sui volunteered to go back and have a word with the king. When the king realized that he was being approached a lowly retainer, he roared at Mao Sui to get out. Mao Sui took a step forward and put his hand on his sword. 'You only talk like that because you've got a big army and a lot of bodyguards,' he said. 'But I'm right beside you now and your life is in my hands. Your bodyguards are no good to you because they're not close enough to stop me. It's time to start listening.' He explained that if the king did not join the Zhao against the Qin, the Qin would defeat the Zhao, and the Chu would be next. The king was impressed with this argument. He joined forces with Pingyuan and together they saved Handan.

32. Han Xin (韓信, c.231–196 BCE) rose from poverty to become a great military general and one of the founders of the Han dynasty. As a young man suffering from hunger, he was given rice by a poor woman, and offered to pay her back when he had made his fortune. She told him not to worry about it. Many years later, he became King of Chu, at which point he returned to her village and repaid her with gold.

33. Hu Zongxian (胡宗憲, 1512–65) is, along with Từ Hải, one of two characters in the story who have a real-life avatar (see the Introduction, pp. xxxv–xliv). In the official accounts, he is given credit for defeating the pirate Xu Hai in 1556 and for eliminating the pirate

chief Wang Zhi a couple of years later. The official records give a different story of events from the story we find in *Jīn Yún Qiáo Zhuàn*, however, and the character in *The Song of Kiều* should be considered fictional rather than a portrait of the historical person. The real Hu Zongxian's direct descendant, Hu Jintao (胡錦濤, born 1942), was President of China from 2003 to 2013.

34. Kiều's reference is to Huang Chao (835–84), whose ultimately doomed rebellion severely weakened the Tang dynasty.

35. Borges calls this Taoist fable (of the man who dreamed of being a butterfly, and on waking was unsure whether he was now a butterfly dreaming he was a man) the finest metaphor of all. He notes that, immediately after waking, life always has something dreamlike about it; and also that the butterfly is the perfect choice of creature for the image, being delicate and evanescent, 'unlike tigers, typewriters or whales'.

36. Dou Yujun, a selfish young man from Jizhou, was childless at thirty years old when his grandfather came to him in a dream. 'Your time is up,' said his grandfather's ghost. 'You have less than a year to live. The only way to change your destiny is to change your ways.' Dou Yujun took this advice and started helping others. After a few months, his grandfather returned in another dream, explaining that his good deeds had brought him thirty-six more years, and that he would now be granted five brilliant sons. (In other words, he should have died at sixty-six. However, the story also records that he died peacefully at the age of eighty-two, having said goodbye to his relatives; it doesn't explain where the extra sixteen years came from.) Compare Dickens' *A Christmas Carol* (1843). This tale appears in a Ming-era collection; it supposedly derives from the Song dynasty (960–1279).

37. For help with this translation, as with so much of the background information for this edition of *Kiều*, I am greatly indebted both to Eric Henry and to Guanlin Li. All mistakes, of course, are mine alone.

Acknowledgements

I am grateful for the Hawthornden Fellowship which in 2009 enabled me to complete the first draft of *The Song of Kiều*; in the previous year, my version of the opening lines won a Stephen Spender Prize for Poetry in Translation. Extracts from the poem have also appeared in *Poetry Review* ('The Wooing of Kiều by Kim'; 99/2, 26–30) and in *Modern Poetry in Translation* ('Kiều Arrives at the Brothel of Lâm-Tri'; 3/13, 81–5).

The manuscript's first reader was my father, Len Allen (1931–2009), who sadly never lived to find out how this story ends. David and Helen Constantine provided encouragement and support when I was initially preparing extracts for publication. Professor Eric Henry, the (now retired) Senior Lecturer in Asia Studies at the University of North Carolina and, more recently, the (also retired) East Asian scholar Charles Benoit, have been incredibly generous throughout this process with their time and expertise. The tracing of the origins of the Kiều myth, in particular, owes a great deal to their painstaking research into Chinese and Vietnamese primary source materials. My other great collaborator has been my friend Guanlin Li (李冠林), Deputy Director of Dongying Campus at the China University of Petroleum (中国石油大学), whose boundless enthusiasm for research helped answer so many of my questions, no matter how obscure, and whose knowledgeable enthusiasm for the culture (and especially the music) of classical East Asia has given the introduction and notes to this poem a far greater richness than I could have achieved alone. I would also like to thank my University of Liverpool students – too numerous to mention individually – especially those from Vietnam, China and Japan, for their many comments and suggestions while I was preparing these notes.

For the maps, Karl Baxter at Stunn and Mike Davis and Jeff Edwards at Penguin have done a highly professional job of turning my scant sketches into clear and detailed visual aids. I would like to thank everybody at Penguin who has helped put this book together, but especially my editor, Henry Eliot, who was curious enough to root out this version of *The Song of Kiều* in the first place, who has since championed it through the publication process, and who has always proved such a patient and generous editor. Finally, I would like to thank my wife Ann, and my children Oisín and Molly, for their patience while I worked on this book.

THE SONGS OF THE SOUTH

An Ancient Chinese Anthology of Poems by Qu Yuan and Other Poets

'From of old things have always been the same:
Why should I complain of the men of today?'

Chu chi (*The Songs of the South*) and its northern counterpart, *Shi jing*, are the two great ancestors of Chinese poetry and contain all we know of its ancient beginnings. *The Songs of the South* is an anthology first complied in the second century AD. Its poems, originating from the state of Chu and rooted in Shamanism, are grouped under seventeen titles. The earliest poems were composed in the fourth century BC and almost half of them are traditionally ascribed to Qu Yuan. Covering subjects ranging from heaven to love, work to growing old, regret to longing, they give a penetrating insight into the world of ancient China, and into the origins of poetry itself.

Translated with an Introduction and Notes by David Hawkes

ISBN: 978 0 14 119 870 5

AS I CROSSED A BRIDGE OF DREAMS

Lady Sarashina

'I lie awake,
Listening to the rustle of the bamboo leaves,
And a strange sadness fills my heart'

As I Crossed a Bridge of Dreams is a unique autobiography in which the anonymous writer known as Lady Sarashina intersperses personal reflections, anecdotes and lyrical poems with accounts of her travels and evocative descriptions of the Japanese countryside. Born in 1008, Lady Sarashina felt an acute sense of melancholy that led her to withdraw into the more congenial realm of the imagination – this deeply introspective work presents her vision of the world. While barely alluding to certain aspects of her life such as marriage, she illuminates her pilgrimages to temples and mystical dreams in exquisite prose, describing a profound emotional journey that can be read as a metaphor for life itself.

Translated with an Introduction by Ivan Morris

ISBN: 978 0 14 044 282 3

THE TALES OF ISE

'Was it you who came to me,
or I who went to you?
I cannot tell.
Was I awake or sleeping?
Was it real, or just a dream?'

The Tales of Ise is one of the most famous and important works
of Japanese literature. Consisting of 125 poem tales loosely based
on the life of the hero, Narihira, a model lover of the Heian period,
they evoke a world in which beauty and refinement were a way
of life. Covering such themes as forbidden love, devotion between
friends and pleasure in nature, these lyrical episodes combine great
elegance with a subversive, experimental wit. This delightful,
groundbreaking translation brings out the sophisticated humour
and playfulness of the original, which has inspired Japanese art
and literature for a millenium.

Translated with a Commentary by Peter Macmillan
Foreword by Donald Keene

ISBN: 978 0 14 139 257 8